THE BEST OF FRIENDS

Jill Ross Klevin

D1135864

SCHOLASTIC INC.
New York Toronto London Auckland Sydney Tokyo

For Adam and Sloane,
two of my best friends

Cover Photo by Owen Brown

ISBN 0-590-33782-3

12 11 10 9 8 7 6 5 4 3 2 1   1   5 6 7 8/8 0/9

Printed in the U. S. A.   06

THE BEST OF FRIENDS

A Wildfire Book

WILDFIRE TITLES
FROM SCHOLASTIC

—— *1* ——

"**Y**ou *can't always judge a book by its cover.*"

My father, who is prone to uttering all these trite sayings at the drop of a hat, used to say that to me all the time, but I never realized how true it was until I got to know Susannah Ellis. Not only is Susannah Ellis walking proof of how on target that particular corny cliché really is, she's also the person who totally transformed my life. Until she came along to do that, my life was pretty dull by anybody's standards.

To say she and I were complete opposites would be an understatement. We couldn't have been more different if we'd tried. We had absolutely nothing whatsoever in common, didn't know one another, didn't think we ever would. Oh, sure, we lived in the same town, Tarzana; in the same state, California. We went to the same school and had some of the same classes, but that was where the similarities ended. If you had told me back then that we'd wind up friends, I would have said you were losing your marbles, that such a thing was totally impossible. However, that was before the advent of Careers Day and the divine intervention of Dorothea Dorcas.

Dorothea Dorcas was my eleventh-grade social science teacher. Her idea of a creative learning experience was to trot the class down to Numero Uno Pizzeria on Ventura Boulevard to watch Phil Esposito flip pizza dough in the air and listen to him yell at his wife. Only someone totally out of touch with reality would dream up a project like Careers Day, then compound the felony by setting up committees to work on said project, putting two people as disparate as the reigning class beauty queen and the official class genius on the same committee. (Susannah Ellis was the former, so you know what that made *me*, The Girl Brain. Not the image I dreamed of projecting to the world at large, but I was stuck with it, unfortunately. Luckily, it was tempered to some degree by my reputation for being funny, nutty, outspoken, and honest.)

It was my impression at that particular point that Susannah Ellis was the walking epitome of that age-old stereotype, the girl who's beautiful but dumb. If every time a teacher calls on a person, she responds with, "I don't know," or "I don't understand the question," or "I couldn't find time to do the assignment," even the least prejudicial person will tend to come to that conclusion, so I don't really feel I was being prejudiced.

When I say Susannah Ellis was beautiful, I

don't mean she was just another of your average, everyday, garden variety pretty girl like a lot of pretty girls who are walking around today; like my older sister Andrea, for instance, who, although she is one of your prettier pretty girls, isn't anywhere *near* Susannah Ellis's league. Susannah wasn't just beautiful. She was gorgeous, the kind of gorgeous that, when she walked into a room, everybody stopped whatever they were doing and stared at her. Just imagining what it must feel like to walk around looking like Susannah Ellis gave me goosebumps. If you had asked me, at that point in my life, who in the entire world I most wanted to look like, without hesitation I would have told you, "Susannah Ellis!" It hadn't escaped me that, if I *did* look like her, a certain boy, who shall remain nameless for the time being, would not be able to help but notice that I was a girl and not just one of the boys.

Susannah wasn't just tall. She was *statuesque*. She wasn't just graceful. She was as graceful as a ballerina. She didn't just have a good body. Hers was perfection, a ten-plus-plus. She didn't have just plain blue eyes, but violet-blue ones — large, luminous eyes like limpid pools the heroines in those soppy romantic novels always have. Her nose was perfect. Her skin was flawless. You knew it would never have the affrontery to break out. Her hair was not only naturally blonde right down to its roots, it was also long, thick, lustrous, and did anything she told it to do, and every day she came to school with it in a different style. She didn't wear just plain clothes like the rest of us. She

3

wore costumes, ensembles, gorgeous outfits you knew came from the most expensive boutiques around.

The day Ms. Dorcas announced the Careers Day project was a Wednesday. I know because I have my violin lessons on Wednesdays, and I had one that day. Susannah walked in wearing black silk baggy trousers, a cerise wool jacket with padded shoulders and a black lizard cowboy belt, a Hawaiian shirt, black with fruits all over it, and unreal cowboy boots, black leather with red top-stitching. With her hair swept to one side, secured with a flowered comb, her makeup so professional-looking, she looked like some sort of high fashion model on her way to a photography session, as though she had just stepped off the cover of *Vogue* or *Mademoiselle*. She made the other girls invisible.

"She thinks she's one of Charlie's Angels," Trisha Sperling muttered to me, being her usual warm and loving self.

"Her family must be loaded," Jeannine Price said, staring at Susannah. "She spends a fortune on clothes."

"She's just so vain, it's disgusting!" Lori Metzger said, glancing at Trisha for approval. Trisha was looking at Susannah as though she would like to stab her to death with her ballpoint pen.

"I'm dying for one of those Hawaiian shirts," Franny Freeman drooled, looking awestruck. "You can say whatever you like about her. I'd be snobby, too, if I looked like that."

4

"Not too shabby," I agreed, wishing Marshall Medford would move his burly self out of the way so I could get a look at Bobby Stern to see whether his tongue was hanging out or not. Before the cat session could get off the ground, Ms. Dorcas came in and started taking attendance. Then she launched into a long-winded explanation of this project the class was about to embark on; Careers Day, she called it, passing out mimeographed instruction sheets that outlined the whole project in detail, explaining what we were supposed to do. It wasn't a big boost to her ego when her explanation was greeted with groans, moans, grumbles, and a general overall negative attitude from those assembled. Being an unremittingly positive person, and totally out of touch with what was going on in class or out of it, Ms. Dorcas didn't let herself become affected by all that negativism, as some teachers would. She just went blithely on, so enthusiastic about her project she was practically hyperventilating. She explained it in excruciatingly boring detail, despite the fact that the mimeos told us everything we needed to know, droning on and on at great length in that awful monotone voice of hers that practically puts you to sleep, sounding like the taped instructions you have to listen to prior to taking an I.Q. test or an S.A.T. You know, like when this person tells you in a singsong voice, "*You will now pick up your pencils and open your test booklets to page one. Do not begin until your teacher gives the signal, then start with question one, page one,*" etc., etc., etc.

"I have assigned you all to committees," she

said. Everyone really flipped out at that. I mean, *committees*? We used to do that back in second grade. "Next Thursday you will have the day off from school . . ." (That was better. Less moaning and groaning, more shouts of "Right on!", "Way to go!", and "Far out!") ". . . by which time you will have selected someone, one of your parents, with whom you will spend that day gathering information for an in-depth report to the class on his, or her, profession or career."

"This is dumb!" I whispered to Franny Freeman who was sitting across the aisle.

"She's trying to do away with the generation gap," Franny whispered back. "Foster a little family togetherness and intercommunication."

"Does it have to be a parent?" Loren Michaels asked. Dorcas said yes, she would prefer that it was, and he added, "What if you don't *have* one?", whereupon Ms. Dorcas started doing this whole number about how there were lots of kids who actually didn't, so we should not be so insensitive as to make a joke out of such a tragic situation. I felt like a rat for having laughed.

I won't deny the concept of a project centered on somebody's profession or career didn't fascinate me. Not only that, but I deeply resented having to squander my precious time on an assignment that I knew was going to turn out to be a time waster. Also, I resented the idea of working on a committee, something I have never liked because, frankly, I work best independently. I don't need other people slowing me down, giving me hassles. Usually I'm the one who winds up doing all the work. They wind up getting a free ride and my A-plus.

If I thought I was unthrilled at *that* point in the proceedings, wait. Things got steadily worse as they went along, and when Ms. Dorcas started calling out the names of the people on the committees, I *really* got depressed.

"Committee number three," she sang out, and I swear she was looking straight at me and gloating, "Allison Lawrence, Marshall Medford, Robert Stern, and Susannah Ellis."

"Lucky you!" Franny Freeman whispered.

"Want to trade?" Trisha Sperling inquired, giving me a jab in the shoulder blade with her pen. I told her I'd be beside myself with joy if only we could, but of course both of us knew Ms. Dorcas was too rigid to allow any shifting around of committee members. It was common knowledge, because Trisha never stopped talking about it, that she was madly in love with Marshall Medford, The Boy Hulk. A lot of good it would have done her to switch committees. Muscles Medford was in love with one person and one person only, *himself*.

I sat there chewing my lip, sending Ms. Dorcas mental messages of doom. Putting me on the same committee with Medford, Stern, and Ellis, The Beautiful People of Leland High, was like putting Alfred Einstein together with The Osmonds.

"I feel like I'm back in third grade," Bobby Stern commented as he passed my desk.

"Ms. Dorcas was a third-grade teacher once,"

I mumbled, getting up and following him out of the room. Our committee met in the corridor. I stood there watching Susannah undulate towards me, fervently wishing I had had the foresight to wear something to school besides my scrungiest Levis and that holey, old sweatshirt I had inherited from my sister. Should I fake a massive migraine? A fainting spell? An appendicitis attack so I could spend the rest of the period safe in the nurse's office, or just crawl into the nearest corner and suck my thumb?

Marshall leered lasciviously at Susannah. "You look like a luscious fruit salad," he said to her. "Don't fight it, babe. I know you're madly in love with me."

Susannah gave him this look that ought to have turned him into a mass of quivering jelly, but Marshall didn't even notice. Marshall is endowed with about as much depth and sensitivity as a stone statue. He pretends to be very sure of himself, but I think a lot of that is an act. Sometimes I get the distinct impression he's just the opposite of sure. If he really felt all that terrific about himself, would he have to swagger around, acting macho.

"I don't understand what we're supposed to do," Susannah was saying, looking confused. "What's this project about anyway?"

"Here. Read all about it," I said, handing her my mimeo, since she didn't seem to have one of her own. This was going to be the pits, I just knew it. Not only was I stuck with The Boy Hulk, but I was going to have to cope with Susannah Stunning, too, the proverbial dumb blonde. Bobby,

8

well, not only was he smart, handsome, and loaded with personality, he was also sensitive and warm. . . . I could go on and on, but suffice it to say that, in *my* estimation, he was the next thing to perfection, and being anywhere in his company would have been sheer heaven for me.

"I still don't get it," Susannah said, handing me back the mimeo. "Does she want us to spend the day following somebody around, watching them staple papers together and take coffee breaks? Is *that* what she wants us to do?"

"I think that's the general idea, yes," I murmured, fighting the urge to be sarcastic. Let's face it, if this project were any more simpleminded, it would be Mother Goose. So how come Susannah was having all this trouble understanding it? What was so complex and complicated?

She smiled at me, nearly knocking me flat with those dazzling white teeth of hers. I tried telling myself it would be pretty tragic to be that dumb, but it didn't make me feel one bit better. It didn't help either that Bobby was looking at her as though she were a dream come true.

Parents are always trying to convince you looks aren't all that important, that it's what's *inside* that counts. I'm here to tell you, that's pure baloney! The kids in your class aren't about to elect you Most Popular Girl on the basis of your wit, your innate sensitivity, or your Iowa test scores, and boys aren't falling all over themselves wanting to date you because you get A's in Trigonometry, know what *Roget's Thesaurus* is, or how to speak fluent French.

Take me, for instance, the prime example of the

above theory at work. *Inside* I was really super, definitely way above average in the brains, wit, and sensitivity departments. But did it enable me to get what I wanted out of life? Definitely not. Because, with all that going for me, I didn't have looks, and looks are what matters, at least where kids my age are concerned. Okay, I wasn't ugly, but I wasn't pretty either. Or even attractive. The fact is, I was sort of a girl nothing, a *blah*, and where boys and dates and popularity were concerned, that made me the proverbial invisible girl.

Let me explain what I mean by *blah*. *Blah* is another word for plain. My face was a blob, for one thing. Other girls had heart-shaped faces, oval faces, round ones. Mine was just pudgy. My nose wasn't even a nose, just two nostrils surrounded by an array of horrendous freckles. My eyes were okay, I guess, green, sizable, but hiding out behind a pair of horn-rimmed glasses, who could see them? Since I couldn't see a thing without them, I couldn't see my way clear to dispensing with them. I wasn't *that* anxious to be attractive. My hair, well, frazzly's a good word. Not only frazzly and impossible to do anything with, but mouse-brown, too. My body? We won't go into that. It's too depressing.

"Well," you're probably saying along about now, "if you think you're such a mess, why not *do* something about improving your looks?"

Don't think I wouldn't if I could. But no way are you going to take a pudgy, pear-shaped girl with no chest and turn her into a svelte, slender, striking sex symbol, which is what I yearned to be.

10

There's no sense beating around the bush. I might as well tell it like it is. Although I pretended to be above it all, not interested in superficial things like clothes and boys, parties and an active social life, it was just an act. Deep down underneath I wasn't as dedicated to developing my brain as I made out. In fact, I would gladly have traded it in a flash for a great body and a super face like Susannah Ellis's. That is, if it would have gotten me the boy of my dreams, Bobby, B for Beautiful, Stern!

—— 2 ——

"What lucky parent are we gonna do our report on?" Marshall said, flexing at us. He took a pack of gum out of his pocket, stuffed two sticks in his mouth, then put the pack back without even bothering to offer us any. You always got the feeling Marshall bought his clothes three sizes too small in order to show off all his bulging biceps and triceps. Marshall's prime motivation in life, next to cultivating girls, is cultivating his muscles.

"Do any of our parents have interesting careers?" I asked, watching him make the muscle in his upper arm dance and jiggle. "Let's not pick anyone who does something draggy, you guys. We have to spend the whole, entire day with them, and it'd be a downer having to spend the day locked up in a dentist's office, watching cavities get filled."

"Or a pizza-maker like Phil Esposito," Susannah said, grinning at me.

"Mmm, yes, that certainly was another one of Dorcas's more enlightening projects," I said, shaking my head.

"I guess I *could* ask my dad if we could do the report on *him*," Bobby said, looking as though he'd really rather not.

"A football coach?" Marshall sniggered. "You want to do the report on a day in the life of a football coach? That's not a career. It's a hobby!"

"Some hobby," Bobby said, looking at Marshall as though he thought he was some kind of idiot or something. "Listen, Marshall, my dad had to go through plenty of tough training, and he's worked his butt off to get where he is. He's one of the best college coaches in the country. He coaches a top team, and he gets paid a lot of bread for doing it, too, so I wouldn't exactly call it his hobby."

"Aw, come *on*, Bob. It's not exactly like *work*." Marshall started putting Bobby's dad down. It really got me mad.

I smiled real sweetly at him and asked, "What does *your* father do for a living, Marshall?"

His face got kind of red. He started making all these stupid comments, supposedly humorous ones, trying to wriggle out of answering my question.

"So? What does he do?" I said. "Are you going to tell us, or aren't you?"

"Uh, well, he owns a fleet of trucks," Marshall said, obviously pleased with himself for coming up with such a clever way to avoid the issue.

"What *kind* of trucks?" I asked. I knew darned well what kind, since one of those trucks showed up at our house twice a week, every Tuesday and Thursday, like clockwork.

Marshall's face was practically purple. He looked like he was about to have a fit. "Uh, refuse removal," he said in a choked voice.

"You mean *garbage*?" Bobby said and burst out laughing. Marshall looked as though he would have liked the floor to open up underneath him and swallow him up. I would have felt sorry for him, except he had it coming.

"Well, that takes care of the guys," I said, smiling at Susannah. "So, what does your dad do?" I added, figuring she'd probably tell me her old man owned half of Beverly Hills or something.

"My parents are divorced. My father doesn't live here anymore. He moved to Oregon. He runs a nursery."

"You mean a school for little kids?" Marshall asked.

She shook her head and replied, "No, a place where they grow and sell plants. You know, a nursery," in a halting voice.

This was a definite shocker. I mean, who would have thought, from the general message this girl sent out, that her dad wasn't at least a tycoon, and that she'd be embarrassed about what he did for a living? Or about anything having to do with herself, for that matter.

"Okay, scratch fathers, you guys," I said, feeling kind of embarrassed myself. "Moving right along here, let's go on to mothers. I know it's hard to believe, but *they* happen to be people, too, just like fathers. Some of them even have

14

careers, would you believe? Being that Dorcas is such a militant women's libber, us doing our report on a mom, instead of a dad, might just possibly get us a higher grade."

"Well, my mother doesn't work," Marshall said, making it obvious he thought nobody's should.

"Mine either," Bobby put in, "at least not since she had the baby."

"Your mom had a *baby*?" Susannah breathed, looking at him as though he had just grown a pair of wings and a halo.

"Yeah, unless the stork brought him," Bobby replied. "Hey, Al, that reminds me, your mom's the baby doctor."

"Uh-uh, that's my dad. *He's* the pediatrician. *She's* the neurosurgeon."

It seemed to be Susannah's day for surprising revelations. She stared at me as though I'd just announced my parents were the king and queen of England. To tell the truth, I can never understand why people think that's so impressive, having parents who are doctors. I mean, aside from the fact that some of them make a mint of money, what's so terrific about being a doctor? Or having parents who are? I mean, think about it, there must be virtually tons of people who are parents *and* doctors, and vice versa.

Do you have any idea what it's like, being the offspring of two super-dedicated physicians, both of whom are bent on curing all the ills of humanity at large? Well, for one thing, scratch family togetherness. That's out, because everytime you plan an outing, or even a dinner, zappo! Emer-

15

gency strikes. Either some dumb kid drives his little tricycle into a brick wall or swallows something lethal; or somebody is suddenly in dire need of brain surgery, my mother's particular forté. You always get cancelled out, and you never get an uninterrupted night's sleep, because those beepers of theirs are beeping away, day and night. If I had a choice, I'd have chosen anything else for parents, even refuse removal engineers, like Marshall's father, rather than doctors. At least then, every once in a while, there'd be half a chance I'd get to see them.

"Sorry, people, but my parents are out. It's unethical, for one thing. For another, I don't think you guys would dig spending the day in my dad's office, hearing the pitiful shrieks and agonized screams of a host of horrible little monsters; nor do I imagine you'd enjoy accompanying Mother into the operating room at Tarzana General to watch her probe the interior of someone's brain."

"Oh, I don't know. Sounds like fun," Bobby said.

Susannah looked as though she was going to throw up any minute. "How can she *do* that?"

"Veeery carefully," Bobby grinned.

"Ugh! I could never be a doctor, not in a million years."

I smiled at her, thinking, *No kidding! You must be putting me on,* and said, "What about your mother? Does she work?"

Susannah nodded. "For this lawyer in Encino, only he's a divorce lawyer, and you know what that means."

"No, what?" Marshall asked.

"Well, his clients are convinced everyone is a private detective hired by their exes to spy on them." She went on to tell us about her mother's boss and how he had this fixation about strict secrecy, so naturally we couldn't use him for our report. I remember thinking that this was the first time I had ever heard Susannah say more than three words in succession, except for "May I be excused" and "I don't understand the question." I caught myself wondering whether she was really as uptight as she seemed, or if I was just projecting. It was hard to believe someone who looked as together as Susannah Ellis could be uptight in any situation, social or otherwise. Until now, I had always gotten the impression she was Ms. Cool, but now she seemed self-conscious, even shy. It really caught me off guard.

Bobby said, "Hey, this is terribly fascinating, really, but it's not getting us much of anywhere with this project. We've got to dream up somebody to do the report on. Come on, people. Think!"

"I'm thinking," I said, pushing my glasses back up my non-nose. They just slipped right back down again. "One of these days I'm going to break down and get myself some contact lenses," I said, pushing them back up.

The end-of-period bell rang. We all took off in different directions, promising each other we'd give the problem our undivided attention overnight and come to school with something by the morrow. As they walked away, I heard Bobby say to Susannah, "Well, at least you're on my committee."

Just what my already damaged ego needed. You know that awful sinking feeling you get when you have your heart set on something and want it so desperately? More desperately than you've ever wanted anything in your whole life? And suddenly you realize it's hopeless, that you'll never get it? That's how I felt at that moment, watching the two of them walk away, looking so perfect together, the perfect couple, like in that TV commercial, the one with the boy and girl in the soft drink ad, frolicking on the beach. Mentally, I aimed my handy dandy laser gun at Susannah's rear and fired, but she didn't vanish into thin air as I was hoping. She just kept on going down the corridor, leaving me standing there staring after her, feeling like the least desirable girl in the world.

—— *3* ——

That night turned out to be one of those rare nights when my parents and I wound up having dinner at the same time and place for a change. In our house, the chances of that happening are about forty to one. So I was delighted when my violin lesson was over, and I was saying good-bye to my teacher, Jackie, at the front door, to see both my parents' cars pull into the driveway.

"Hey, don't I know you?" I said to my father when he walked in the door. "And you," to my mother, "the lady with the freckles and the curly, red hair? You look familiar, too."

"Don't you know me? I'm your mother!" my mom exclaimed, making like a heroine from a 1940s movie about a long-lost mother and her child, reunited. She sniffed the air. "What's that I smell? Roast beef? No wonder my grocery bills are so exorbitant! Helga may be the best housekeeper in America, but she certainly isn't the most economical shopper."

"Well, it's a treat, seeing you guys, let me tell you," I said, following them into the kitchen, where Helga was basting a rib roast big enough for the whole Russian army.

"The feeling's mutual, whoever you are," my dad said, heading for the refrigerator to get the wine. He went to the cabinet to get two glasses, peering into the pots on the stove along the way. "Someday, daughter dear, in about fifty years, when you're where we are right now, you'll look back and say, 'Dear old mom and dad! I understand now why they never got home for dinner.' "

"Hey, I understand right now," I said to him, grabbing a piece of lettuce from the salad bowl on my way to set the table. "The thing is, I'm not going to be like you guys, so dedicated it hurts. I'm going to find time for a few more things than healing humanity. Things like traveling and being with my family."

"Famous last words!" he said, pouring wine for my mom and himself. He handed her a glass. She took a sip, closed her eyes, and sighed appreciatively. "I've been thinking about this all day, getting home for a nice, leisurely dinner, just the three of us."

Honestly, it felt like a holiday, real festive and special, and just because the two of them had come home for dinner instead of staying at the hospital or eating out in a rush. I don't mean to sound like a momma's or daddy's girl, but it did get lonely sitting there having dinner every night with Helga. It was better when my sister Andrea

20

was home. Then at least it was Helga, plus Andrea. Now, with old Andrea off at Berkeley taking pre-med, the house was like a morgue most of the time. Not that I don't love Helga. I do! She's wonderful. She's loving, caring, faithful, steadfast, amusing, and strong. She's even the world's greatest cook, but scintillating she is not. Trying to make dinner table conversation with Helga is like conversing with a stone wall. Besides, what was the use of her creating all those culinary concoctions every night just so the two of us could sit down opposite each other at the table and eat them alone? It made her feel unappreciated, cooking sumptuous repasts for two instead of four, and all that effort was certainly wasted on me. Without my folks there to share the dinner with, I would just as well have settled for canned soup and a sandwich.

Their never being around had never seemed to bother Andrea the way it did me, but then Andrea had never been around much herself. Ms. Popularity always had so much going on in her life, she was booked solid seven nights a week, fifty-two weeks a year. You wouldn't think someone like Andrea would be so dedicated to the idea of being a member of the medical profession, but she was. I, who was just the type you would expect to be, wasn't all that sure. Of course, I hadn't mentioned that disturbing fact to my parents as yet. Didn't think I ever would either. The idea of there not being *four* Doctor Lawrences would have been too much for them to handle, given the fact that they had been dreaming of passing the doctoring tradition along, just

21

as it had been passed along to them by their parents; rather, their fathers, since those were pre-women's lib days.

"If Mom and Dad told you they didn't want you to be a doctor, you'd be dying to be one," Andrea had said to me once, trying to convince me my doubts derived from adolescent rebelliousness. I wasn't sure she was wrong. I was willing to keep an open mind on the subject. In any case, lately I had been having the most disturbing thoughts on the subject; thoughts I needed to explore, but everytime I tried to talk to my parents about them, I wound up chickening out, not wanting to upset them.

I finished setting the table. Helga announced that dinner was ready, and we all sat down.

"So, how's school?" my father said, turning into a parent before my eyes.

I shrugged. "Same as usual," I replied, filling him in on the latest from good old Leland, including Ms. Dorcas's fiasco, Careers Day.

"Maybe there's more to it than meets the eye," my dad said, lapsing into another cliché.

"Speaking of eyes," I mumbled, pushing my glasses up my nose, "Mom, I think I ought to get contact lenses. These glasses won't stay up. They're driving me crazy. Besides, they make me look like a speckled owl."

My dad, who has always been my best audience, burst out laughing. My mother smiled her inscrutable smile and said, "Anytime you're ready, let me know, and I'll call Dr. Koenig for an appointment."

"Do you think I ought to get them?" I inquired, hoping she'd take a stand one way or the other.

She reached for the bowl of potatoes. "We'll ask Dr. Koenig what he thinks, then you can make your own decision. After all, they're your eyes."

I nodded, feeling let down. That's my mom, so into letting me be myself, it's disgusting. Just once I'd love her to give an opinion, issue an ultimatum, say *something* besides, "It's your decision."

I helped myself to a hot roll, inundating it with butter, and listened to my dad discoursing on the relative merits of glasses versus contact lenses, going on at great length, giving arguments for both in an equally objective manner. My father is definitely the professional type, at least lookswise, in his tweed jackets with elbow patches, his horn-rimmed glasses, and his flannel slacks. He looks like the typical stereotype of the college professor, right down to his pipe and tobacco pouch. But, as he is always saying, looks can be deceiving. He can be pretty dry and didactic, but sometimes he can surprise you and do something totally out of character. Sometimes I get the feeling that inside that uptight, middle-American exterior, there's a crazy kid waiting to get out.

My mom, on the other hand, is a definite throwback to the fifties with her sensible dresses and sensible shoes, and her sensible attitudes, some of which date back to the dark ages, not even the fifties. She may think, act, and dress middle-aged, but she really looks young with her reddish-blonde hair cut short in curls, and her face that, especially when she smiles, looks like the face of a teenager, pug nose, freckles, green eyes, and all. Lucky Andrea had inherited her features, her hair, and her body, only Andrea was an improvement on the old family recipe. All I'd inherited were Mom's green eyes.

My father was still going on, exploring every possible aspect on the contact lenses-versus-glasses controversy. "So, Dad," I said, debating with myself over whether or not I wanted that second piece of roast beef, "do you think I ought to get contact lenses, or don't you?"

He smiled and said, "That's up to you, Allison."

See what I mean? You couldn't get a straight answer for love or money. Would it have killed one of them to take a stand, one way or the other? The only thing my mother ever ventured an opinion on were my clothes, and that was the *last* thing I wanted her advice on, being that she was the type who thought blue jeans were these things you only wore to do the gardening.

"I'll never understand why you insist on wearing those disreputable blue jeans," she was always saying. "And that sweatshirt! Allison, really. You should have thrown it away months ago. It's threadbare."

"So, what's for dessert?" I said, getting up and starting to clear the table.

"What you see is what you get," Helga said when I walked into the kitchen. She was spooning raspberry sherbet over fresh fruit cup. "Your mother says no more fattening desserts. We're all going on a diet."

24

"I may run away from home!"

"Wait! I'll go with you."

"Mom, if you don't let Helga bake, she'll probably quit," I said, coming back into the dining room, balancing three compote dishes with fruit cup and sherbet in them.

"Probably," my mom said, and smiled serenely at me. "After twenty years, it's time. Listen, help a poor mother out, will you? I must take off some weight, and I'm not going to be able to do that if Helga is constantly baking all those goodies."

"You're not fat at all, Mom," I said, digging into my so-called dessert. "What you need is exercise, that's all. You ought to join that new health club that opened up in the Promenade."

When I was helping Helga with the dishes, my father snuck over to me and whispered, "You're sworn to secrecy. That's what I got your mother for our anniversary, a membership to that spa." He took off for his study to bury his nose in a medical journal. My mother was making herself a cup of tea, musing about how she'd just love to be able to join that spa and indulge and pamper herself, but couldn't because she had no time.

"You ought to make time," I said. "You have a good figure, Mom, but, well, you're approaching that age. If you don't watch out, before you know it, you'll have middle-aged spread. If you joined, maybe I could go with you sometimes. There must be a way to work off these pudgy thighs."

"Try walking," Helga said, giving me this look.

"Or running," my mother put in. "It seems to work, running I mean. Everybody I know is doing it."

25

4

My mother has this thing about antiques. She likes everything to be old: furniture, clothes, houses, cars, everything. Her theory is that everything that's new is inferior, and everything that's old is superior. As my father would say, they just don't make things like they used to anymore.

Our house is old. So is all our furniture. And when I say old, I mean ancient. Most of it belonged to my great-great-grandmother. In fact, the furniture in my bedroom was once my mother's mother's when *she* was a little girl. That gives you a general idea of how old it really is. I have to admit, I like my room a lot. It's probably the nicest room in the house. It's so nice my sister Andrea spent ten solid years trying to finagle me out of it and stick me with that cruddy room of hers she decorated herself and turned into a reasonable facsimile of the boys' locker room at school.

My room would probably look a whole lot nicer if I wasn't such a total and complete slob. As my father's always saying, my room always looks like the aftermath of an earthquake, wall-to-wall mess.

Anyway, after dinner I was up there in Bedlamsville, practicing the number I was going to play in the school concert, when Susannah Stunning called. At first I thought I had charmed her with my scintillating wit and sensational personality, but it wasn't that. She was calling to discuss the project.

"I have an aunt who's a teller at California Savings in Encino," she informed me. "She said we could do our report on her."

I didn't want to annihilate her ego, but a day in the life of a bank teller? Watching some lady cash checks all day and make savings account deposits? Not my idea of an uplifting experience! Trying to be diplomatic, I suggested we try and get someone else. We started talking about Ms. Dorcas and her tendency to treat us like third graders, and from there the conversation went on to teachers in general.

"Ms. Hartley's my favorite teacher of all time," I said. "She's the greatest!"

"I love her!" Susannah gushed. "She's so young-looking, and so pretty. I love the way she dresses, don't you? Kind of campy, know what I mean?" She went on to describe every outfit Mickey Hartley had ever worn in intricate detail.

"Who'll we get for that dumb project?" she said. "If we can't use fathers, and your mom and mine are out, and Marshall's and Bobby's are housewives . . ."

"Wait a second. That's *it*," I exclaimed, coming up with a brainstorm. "Being a housewife, that's a career, a non-paying one; sort of a *non-career*. A Day in the Life of an Average American Housewife. How's that for a title? Think about it, she's the most overworked, underappreciated, and certainly most underpaid employee in the country."

"What a fantastic idea!" Susannah said, and we started tossing it around, working out a format for the report that would enable us to keep the identity of our worker secret until after we had made all the points we wanted to make. "You know, it would just be so much more effective if the class didn't know the true identity of our non-career person until the end of the report, at which point, after filling them in on all the salient details, we'd zap them with whose profession we'd been reporting on.

"Now all we have to do is come up with an average American housewife and we're set," I said.

"It's up to Marshall and Bobby, obviously, since our mothers are out."

"I know Bobby's mom. She's a doll. I don't know though. She might not have the time."

"We can but hope," Susannah said. "By the way, did you hear about Seth and Lori? Jeannine told me they're going out."

"They are? What a mismatched twosome," I laughed. "I thought Seth was going with Corinne."

"He was, last week. This week it's Lori. Next week? Who knows?"

We went on rapping about who liked whom, who was going with whom, who wanted to be going with whom, etc., the usual gossip. Finally, Susannah said, "I've got to hang up. We've been on for almost an hour. My mother gets mad if I tie up the phone so long." We said good night. Just before she hung up, she added, "I really enjoyed talking to you, Allison."

"Me, too!" I replied, thinking, *How could I ever have thought she was stuck-up?* When you came down to it, talking to her on the phone was just like talking to any of the other kids. Maybe the image she put out was because of her looks and nothing else. Maybe, in a way, she was discriminated against just as much as, say, a handicapped individual, because you looked at her and made up your mind what she must be like based just on how she looked. Maybe Susannah acted stuck-up because she was on the defensive. Maybe people didn't give her a chance to prove who she really was; just wrote her off after one glance as "Susannah Stunning, Ms. Stuck-up of the Year."

In homeroom next day, some of the kids were discussing the project. Trisha asked me what our committee was going to do, and I told her we hadn't decided yet, figuring that was safer than blurting my idea right out and having her steal it, which she'd been known to do.

"So, how are you getting along with Miss Teenage America?" Trisha asked.

"Fine. She's a nice kid."

"A nice kid?" Lori Metzger giggled, giving her mentor, Trisha, a sideways look to make sure she was on the right track. "That's not exactly how *I'd* describe Susannah Ellis!"

They started tearing Susannah apart like a bunch of jealous cats.

"Did you hear she got *six* invitations to the senior prom and turned them all down flat?" Lori said.

"Maybe she's waiting for you-know-who to ask her," Franny Freeman simpered. *You-know-who?* I thought, wondering who the mystery man could be.

"Speak of the devil!" Trisha whispered just as Bobby walked in the door. I felt my stomach slide slowly down to my toes.

He walked up to me and said, "Aren't you coming? We'll be late for rehearsal."

I took off after him, my face on fire. I wish I could just come right out and ask him, "So, what about Susannah Ellis? Have you got a thing for her or not?" I snuck a peek at his profile. Aside from the fact that he was much taller, of course, and had started shaving, he didn't look all that different than he had back in grade school. Not like some of the guys I know, who change so drastically, you would hardly recognize them. Bobby isn't burly and super-muscley, a jock type like Marshall. He's more the sensitive, aesthetic type, tall and slender, with dark, curly hair and blue eyes. Sometimes I think he's too hand-

30

some. Let's face it, if a girl was going with him, and she wasn't exactly drop-dead gorgeous herself, she could get a complex from everyone commenting on how much better looking he was than she.

"You look tired," I said, smiling at him. "Don't you sleep anymore?"

"Not since Timmy was born. Allison, ever since then, our house is like 'Emergency One'; one trauma after another. I never knew it could be such a hassle, bringing up one little kid. He's always coming down with something, usually at three A.M. Would you explain why, when a baby's teething, his nose runs, his ears get infected, and he runs a high fever?"

"You want *me* to explain? Listen, talk to my father. *He's* the pediatrician."

"But a hundred-and-four fever? Al, that's unreal. I thought I'd have a heart attack last night when Mom took his temperature and the thermometer registered a hundred and four."

"Now you're finding out what it's like to be a mother," I said.

"Yeah, that I could have lived without!" He started filling me in on all of Timmy's latest symptoms. When we got to the auditorium, he opened the door and stepped aside so I could go in first, typical of Leland High's official white knight, the only boy in creation who doesn't know chivalry is dead. We took our places on the stage, Bobby in the woodwind section, along with the two other flutes; me in the strings, first violin. Mr. Petrie came in, and we started tuning up. Then we launched into the Beatles medley, this motley

31

assortment of old Beatles' standards Mr. Petrie had arranged himself that sounded like the music you hear in elevators and dentists' waiting rooms.

I guess a lot of people think it's weird, my wanting to play the violin, but when I'm playing I feel terrific, like Yehudi Menuhin, Issac Stern, and Jascha Heifetz rolled up in one. This sounds nutty, I know, but I think I would be perfectly happy if I could spend the rest of my life standing on some street corner, playing my violin for nickels and dimes.

The violin was my parents' idea initially. I think they thought I needed an outlet, something to channel my energy and take my mind off my problems. To them it must have seemed like a nifty hobby, a great way to relax after a long, hard day cracking the books. Also, when I got older, it would be a good change after a day of delivering babies, removing ruptured spleens, and curing the common cold. Of course, to them, playing the violin could never, by any stretch of the imagination, be considered a legitimate, bonafide profession, say like being a doctor.

After rehearsal, Bobby walked me to my locker so I could put my violin away.

"I wish Mr. Petrie hadn't given me that dumb solo," I said, shoving the violin into my already overstuffed locker and slamming the door. "I hate having to get up in front of a whole auditorium full of people and make a fool of myself."

"Hey, come on, Allison. You're *good*, practically a professional. You're not going to make a fool of yourself, believe me."

"I don't know why, but there's no status in being a girl violinist. People put you down. They'd think more of a girl who could twirl a baton or be a cheerleader."

"People! Since when do you care about *them*?"

I shrugged. "I don't, only it's embarrassing, being a girl violinist."

"So, you should've taken up the tuba, or the cello, or the French horn," he said, grinning at me. "Listen, what're we going to do for that social science project? We're supposed to decide by this afternoon."

"Susannah and I came up with an idea last night," I said, and told him about Non-Careers Day.

"It's good. I like it," he said. "It'll be a satire, kind of like that thing we did last year in English. Remember, when we were studying *Gulliver's Travels*?"

"Right! The whole point would be that, despite all this stuff with women's lib changing things and all, a lot of women in our society are still in that traditional role."

"Who're we going to get though?"

"My mom's out," Marshall said when we asked him during the committee meeting that afternoon. "Thursday's her bridge day."

Susannah, Bobby, and I looked at one another. "Marsh, you sure do make an imbecile of yourself at times," I said. Marshall glared at me, trying to figure out what he had said wrong.

"If there's anyone in *my* house who's a housewife, it's not my mom. It's *me*," Susannah said, looking as though that didn't thrill her terrifically.

33

"My mom's the farthest thing from a housewife a woman can be," I put in. We all looked at Bobby.

He said, "Oh, wow! I'm elected, I guess. Well, look, I can't guarantee anything, but I'll try. My mother only leads three lives all at once, which means she doesn't sit still for two seconds running. I'll use the it'll-be-good-for-Timmy-he-likes-company approach, or maybe the come-on-mom-old-girl-do-it-for-me angle."

I never found out which approach he used. He phoned me that afternoon and said systems were go, that we'd meet at his house Thursday, bright and early. I called Susannah and told her, and she said, "Okay, I'll drive over to your house and pick you up on my way."

"You have your own car?" I asked, hugely impressed. Not that plenty of the kids I know don't have cars, but at that particular point in my life, after taking, and failing, two driver's tests, anyone who could drive impressed me.

"My very own," she said, "bought with my very own money, too."

"How did you manage to get enough money to buy a car?"

"Oh, in the summers I lifeguard over at the Calavaras County Swim and Ye Olde Tennis Club."

"Wow! Posher than posh. You can't even *join* that place unless you can prove you're a millionaire."

"Not quite. I think the initiation fee is about fifty thousand."

34

"Egad! Do they pay you a mint?"

"Well, not really, but I give private swimming lessons, and that's really lucrative."

I don't know what came over me. All of a sudden I heard myself asking her if she wanted to come over a little bit early Thursday morning and have some breakfast with me before we went to Bobby's. She sounded pleased, as though she really wanted to come, and we made a date for nine o'clock. You can't imagine how I regretted that impulse! The minute I hung up the phone, I knew I had made a dreadful mistake. Not because I didn't want to be with Susannah or anything like that. Just that, well, Thursday was Helga's day off, and I don't want to give the impression I'm not a good cook or anything, but whenever I get an urge to create some culinary concoction, everyone in my house suddenly decides to eat out.

My mother wasn't going to be any help. The minute you suggest she whip up a bowl of Jell-O, she gives you the "I'm a surgeon, not a chef" routine. Either I'd have to cook or have the thing catered. I started searching through the microwave cookbook Mom had given Helga for Christmas and came up with something simple, the simplest, most basic kind of breakfast imaginable: cheese omelettes, brown-and-serve sausages, hot rolls (packaged, what else?), all made in the microwave for ease of cooking and cleaning up.

Simple. Basic. Right?

Wrong! The omelettes came out looking and tasting like sponges. The sausages got so overdone they fell apart. The rolls were rubbery and bounced across the table, and the butter, which I'd forgotten to remove from the freezer in advance, was like a rock.

"Sorry about that," I mumbled, watching Susannah redistribute her omelette around on her plate. "I'm not one of the world's great gourmet cooks."

"It's okay. I'm not one of the great eaters. Salad and cottage cheese are the mainstays of my daily diet. I put on weight thinking about food. Most of the time, I have to starve."

"*You* have to starve?" Impossible! People like Susannah Stunning didn't have to diet. They were above such considerations as weight problems, acne, the greasies, and dry, flaky skin. They were perfect.

"I *am* human, you know," she said in all seriousness.

"You could've fooled me!" I said, thinking she meant it as a joke.

"Anyway, I'm into nutrition," she went on, oblivious of my attempt at humor. "And I jog every day. If I didn't, I'd turn into a blimp overnight."

"You jog? Every day?" I looked at that perfect face, that perfect body. "I keep meaning to start, but I never get around to it."

"Once you start, you'll be addicted, not because you'll love it all that much. You won't. But, once you start seeing the results, you'll be hooked. I go every morning before school. If you'd like, I could drive over, and we could go together."

"Oh, well, maybe." I had this mental image of

Susannah, wearing some sensational jogging outfit, jogging along like a real pro, and me, a human
pear in sweatpants and a sweatshirt, bringing up
the rear. Susannah smiled at me. She looked so
beautiful in her pink angora sweater with the
puffed sleeves, and the little lace collar with the
bow, her hair all piled up on top of her head, and
I thought wistfully, *If I looked like that, Bobby
wouldn't be able to resist me!*

My mom staggered in and groped her way
across the kitchen to the coffeemaker for her
morning cup of coffee, without which she doesn't
start to function. She took one look at Susannah
and nearly fell down in a faint. She started giving
Susannah the third degree, very subtle, of course.
Susannah got more uptight by the minute. I could
tell she was embarrassed because her parents were
divorced, and that surprised me because, let's
face it, in this day and age, divorce is no big deal.
Nobody gets uptight about divorce anymore.

My mom looked kind of nifty that day, as I
remember, very tailored and smart, like the career
woman she was, in a rust tweed jacket and skirt,
a man-tailored shirt, and those shoes I hate. Very
sensible. Sensible shoes for a sensible woman. I
wondered what Susannah's mother looked like.
Gorgeous, probably, like Susannah.

My mother complimented Susannah on her outfit. I thought I was hearing things. I mean, my
mom, who thinks getting dressed means covering
your body?

"She thought you were gorgeous," I said when
my mother left. Susannah didn't even react. I re-

member thinking that probably when you walked around looking like Susannah, you heard that so often it didn't mean anything to you anymore.

I was totally nonplussed when she said to me, "I wish just once somebody would see beyond my looks. I'm sick and tired of being Susannah Ellis, pretty but dumb."

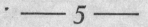

— 5 —

We headed for Bobby's in Susannah's car, a nifty vintage red Mustang convertible.

"Where'd you ever find this car?" I said as we sped along the freeway.

"Oh, this boy I used to go out with, it was his and when he got another one, he sold it to me. I love it, don't you? It's got personality."

"It does," I said wistfully, mentally adding, *And surprisingly enough, so do you!*

Bobby lives in the hills in this big, rambling, old house. You can tell there are lots of kids living there. The yard's always wall-to-wall toys, bicycles, mopeds, motorcycles, and halfway dismantled old cars one of his older brothers is working on. I rang the doorbell. Mrs. Stern opened the door. She looked like a kid herself in cutoffs, a T-shirt, and tennis shoes, with her hair a mess.

"Bobby's still jogging," she said, taking us into

the kitchen. "We'll have some cake and coffee, okay? Do you prefer milk or tea? Bobby drinks herbal tea. I hate it." She started clearing the kitchen table, talking a mile a minute. The table was littered with all these pieces of drawing paper on which were sketches of skinny, scrawny females with no faces in high-styled outfits.

"They're for a course I'm taking at the Fashion Institute," Mrs. Stern explained, dumping all the sketches into this mammoth black leather portfolio with her name lettered on it in gold. "I'm studying to be a fashion designer, you know, or didn't Bobby tell you?"

At the word "fashion," Susannah's ears perked up. The two of them wound up having this lengthy discussion on style, fashion, fabric, sewing, etc., *ad nauseum*, just the sort of thing that turns me off completely, or did then anyway. Finally, thank goodness, Bobby arrived, in jogging shorts and no shirt, with a red bandana tied around his head. I tried not to stare, but he was really attractive. We all sat there having coffee and cake, waiting for Marshall, who called about ten minutes later to announce he wasn't going to be able to make it. Bobby started arguing with him, telling him he'd better or else, but he got a whole lot of nowhere.

"He says his coach called a surprise football practice," Bobby said when he hung up.

"Sure! He was probably going surfing," I grumbled. "He never does any work if he can get somebody else to do it for him, usually some girl who's got a thing for dopes with muscles."

"He's not going to get away with it this time,"

40

Bobby said, reaching for the last piece of cake. "No way are we going to do the work, then share the grade we get with him. If he thinks he's going to get away with that kind of stuff with us, he's wrong. Hey, we'd better get this show on the road, people," he said, glancing at the clock on the wall. "Mom's got to be at school by two, and it's almost eleven-thirty."

"I've never been interviewed before," Mrs. Stern said, getting uptight and nervous. We started asking her all these dumb questions about her life, like what she did every day from the instant she climbed out of bed until she climbed back in at night. How many hours, minutes, and seconds she reckoned she spent doing various household chores, the grocery shopping, the laundry, the cleaning. How she felt about having to do them, etc. It turned out, she was probably the farthest thing from an average American housewife under the sun, mainly because she practically didn't do a stitch of housework.

"Not since the kids got old enough to do it anyway," she said, looking pleased with herself. "They all pitch in together. All I have to do is an occasional tub of laundry and some cooking once in a while. Other than that, I'm a lady of leisure."

"Some lady of leisure!" Bobby said, shaking his head.

Actually Mrs. Stern led the busiest life imaginable. We finally concluded that, if we had to label her, she really was a student; one who just happened to be thirty-nine years old with a six-month-old baby, plus four almost grown-up kids ranging from fifteen to twenty.

41

"How many housewives do you think are thirty-nine, in school, and have babies?" she said.

"Not all that many," I replied, "but that might work out." Already, in my head, I was reworking the original idea, giving it a new slant, a report on a *liberated* American housewife.

We headed upstairs to Bobby's room to work on the report. Bobby's room is the complete antithesis of that cliché of my father's, *You can't judge a book by its cover,* in that it describes Bobby perfectly. One look, and you know what his prime interest in life is, and what his future will probably be. It looks like something straight out of one of those Jacques Cousteau documentaries. Bobby has this thing about whales. He's always going on these whale-watching expeditions. He was going on one the following weekend, he said, down the Baja.

"What do you want to watch whales for?" Susannah asked when he told her about it.

"Whales are fascinating," he replied. Needless to say, once he got started on his favorite subject, we didn't get much done on the report.

"Bobby's so nice," Susannah said when we were driving home to my house. "Not like some of the boys, you know, the macho ones. He's more, well, gentle and sensitive."

"Bobby *is* special," I sighed.

She gave me a look. I just smiled and acted nonchalant. "What should we do about Marshall?" she asked.

"Tell him off. What else?"

"Well, why don't you volunteer," she said, grinning at me. "Being that you're so good with words and all. Hey, are you really a genius, or what? Somebody told me you've got an I.Q. of two hundred."

"Two hundred? Einstein only had about one-fifty. Listen, you know what you said before about being labeled, 'beautiful, but dumb'? I don't like being labeled either, 'plain, but smart.'"

"Sorry! I didn't mean that. Just that you *have* got it all over most of the kids in the smarts department. Don't think you're not pretty impressive; intimidating, too, sometimes. What a vocabulary! Where'd you ever learn all those words anyway? You're a good writer, too. Remember that time in English when we had to study a contemporary writer, then write our own story using that writer's style? When you got up and read that story you wrote? You know, the one about the enchanted island? I flipped. I never heard anything so beautiful. After that, I thought to myself, 'Allison really *is* a genius!' You could be a professional writer, you know it?"

"It's no big deal," I said, and started thinking about what Susannah had said. You suddenly see yourself through somebody else's eyes and it's a shock. I joke a lot about that girl genius thing, but that's just because I'm so defensive about it. Let's face it, nobody wants to be a girl genius. Anyway, I wasn't one, not by any stretch of the imagination.

"You're one person in that school I always liked," Susannah was saying, flooring me completely. "Lots of times I thought it would be great if we could be friends, but I didn't think you'd be interested. I mean, being that you're so intellectual and all."

"Susannah, I don't believe this!" I exclaimed, staring at her. "*You* wanted to be friends with *me*?" I started telling her how I had always been so in awe of her. How I'd thought she was so sophisticated and mature that she'd never want to be friends with any of us lowly kids. For the next half hour we went on telling each other how great each of us thought the other one was.

"It's so easy talking to you," Susannah said. "I don't feel all that comfortable with too many people. I don't have any real friends. That's a drag, not having at least one good, close friend you can really talk to."

"I know. I have the same problem. I used to be real close with this girl Janey, but she moved away, and after that I never got that close with anybody again. I really miss having somebody to confide in, tell things to; things I wouldn't tell to just anyone. The kids at school — Franny, Trisha, Lori, Jeannine — I would never consider them real friends. Just casual acquaintances."

"I know, and you don't tell your innermost secrets to acquaintances. I feel like nobody at that school knows me. They think I'm stuck-up, but they're just so extra sweet to me anyway; even though they really don't like me one bit. I'm sick and tired of having them come on to me and act all phony because they think I'm popular. It's the same thing with boys. Just once I'd like to go out with a boy and know he likes *me*, the *real* me, not the face and the body."

44

"I wouldn't mind having that problem."

She shot me a look. "I never figured you were interested in things like that."

"Things like what?"

"Oh, you know, superficial things, like looks, clothes, and all."

"There's no such thing as a girl who isn't interested in things like that. She may pretend she isn't, but deep down inside, believe me, she is."

I felt like a jerk, being so super honest about something so highly personal and embarrassing, but now that we were baring our souls to one another, I was really letting it all hang out. Truthfully, I didn't even know why, or if I really wanted to.

"Well," Susannah said, pulling into my driveway, "This is just to let you know, in case you don't already, you could be a super-looking girl if you'd pay a little more attention to the way you look and dress."

"Oh, sure. Terrific-looking," I mumbled, my face burning. "Thanks for being diplomatic anyway."

"Hey, wait a second! I realize we don't know each other all that well, but let me clue you in. If there's one thing I'm not, it's a phony. I don't lie. Look," she said, switching off the ignition, turning to me with a warm smile, "nobody just gets up in the morning, washes her face, brushes her teeth, throws on a scuzzy pair of jeans and a sweatshirt, and walks out of the house looking like a model. It takes work. There is no such thing as a natural beauty, Allison. Nobody looks all that great natural, including me."

"That I don't believe!"

"Believe it! Trust me, Allison. I'm not really beautiful. It's just that I know what to do to make the most of myself, that's all. It's no big mystery either. You could learn it, too."

"Me?"

"Why not you? You just have to know what your look is, your style. You've got one. You just haven't gotten in touch with it yet. Look," she added, seeing the dubious look I was giving her, "I'm not saying you're going to be pretty like Lori Metzger is pretty — you know, five-foot-two, eyes of blue; the turned-up nose, the dimples, the whole cutesy-wutesy scene — or like Jeannine is with her sexy, sultry siren bit, but you could be your *own* brand of great-looking. Look, I have a super idea. Why don't I come over here tomorrow after school? I'll bring all my makeup and stuff, and we'll experiment."

"Experiment? You're making me feel like Frankenstein's monster."

"Hey, the nice thing about makeup is, if you don't like the way it comes out, you can scrub it off and start all over again. So? Are we on for tomorrow?"

"Um, yeah. I guess."

After she took off, I was really kicking myself all over the place. I really felt vulnerable, like an open wound. *Why hadn't I just said no when she'd asked me about tomorrow?* I wondered, heading inside.

— 6 —

"Going out tonight?" I said to my mom when we ran into one another in the hallway.

"Yes, to a concert," she replied, looking a little guilty. "Margaret and I have had the tickets for ages."

"Hey, you're entitled to a little recreation for a change, Mom," I said, smiling at her.

"Yes, but I get the feeling you wanted me to stay home tonight. Something on your mind? Do you feel in the mood to talk?"

"No big thing. We'll catch each other some other time."

She smiled. "We haven't had any time together for months, have we? My fault, I admit, but I'm just so busy. I can't seem to fit it all in. Look, maybe this weekend the three of us could do something together. That is, if Daddy and I can work out our schedules at the hospital. I'll ask him, shall I?"

"Sure. That'd be fun!"

She put her arms around me, gave me a kiss on the forehead, smoothed back my hair, and said, "Remember last year, when we went up to Solvang? That was nice, wasn't it?"

I nodded.

"I'll talk to Daddy about the weekend. Maybe we can work something out," she said, giving me another kiss before dashing for the door.

"Well, it can't be helped, I guess. After all, I'm sure you didn't plan it out this way when you decided to devote your life to medicine and become SUPER SURGEON," I called out to her.

A horn honked outside. She fled, and I stood there feeling let down. It was always the same thing. We'd start talking and then she'd have to leave. "Tomorrow," she'd tell me, but every tomorrow just turned into another today, and she was always just too busy, too rushed, too pressured, to take the time. I'd found out the hard way. There never really were any tomorrows. Only todays.

At school next day Franny, Trisha, and some of the other girls, got me cornered and started bombarding me with all these questions about my day with The Beautiful People of Leland High.

"So, how was it?" Trisha said. "Did Marshall do his Arnold Schwarzenegger imitation for you?"

"Marshall didn't even bother to show," I said.

"Really? I bet all you and Bobby did the whole day was sit around watching Susannah put her makeup on," Franny giggled.

"Actually, Susannah and I sat around watching

48

Bobby make like Jacques Cousteau," I replied on the defensive.

Bobby appeared, made a beeline in my direction, and started telling me about this bird sanctuary on an island off Florida somewhere where he might be going over the summer. I could feel all those eyes watching us, hear the girls whispering about us. I pretended to be oblivious, but don't think it didn't bother me. Susannah arrived, on the verge of being late again, as usual. The bell rang, and we all headed for our desks.

"Are you and Bobby having a clandestine affair I don't know about?" she whispered to me.

"Sure, it's so clandestine, even *he* doesn't know about it."

Luci Warner leaned across the aisle and said, "Did you hear about the English exam? Hartley's giving us one next Friday."

Susannah looked at me. "Instant stomach virus," she mumbled.

Obviously Seth Curtis heard her, because he laughed and said, "Yeah, maybe it's catching. Then we can both stay home."

"That'll be the day," I muttered, looking at Seth, who just happened to be Leland's Overachiever of the Year, the most all-around boy in creation, so terrific it made you sick.

I waited until after class, then on the way to first period, I said to Susannah, "What was *that* all about? The instant stomach virus routine, I mean?"

She didn't answer. Just looked at me and said, "What's going on with you and Bobby Stern anyway? I think you really like him."

"Well," I said, starting to get defensive and play it cool, "naturally, I like him. We've been friends ever since kindergarten, for gosh sakes." I saw the look she was giving me, broke down, and mumbled, "Yes. So I like him. So what? Anyway, is it that noticeable?"

"I'm just extra perceptive, that's all. Why does it have to be such a deep, dark secret, Allison? Would it be such a tragedy if the boy knew how you felt?"

"Are you kidding?" I gave her a horrified look. "Susannah, can you think of anything more humiliating than to have a boy you're madly in love with find out you're madly in love with him when he's not even mildly madly in love with *you*?"

"You lost me somewhere around the first madly in love. But how do you know Bobby doesn't feel the same way you do?"

"Susannah, if he did, wouldn't he have done something about it by now? Bobby Stern thinks of me as just one of the guys. He even calls me Al most of the time."

"I know, but that's no indication. I mean, I get the feeling Bobby's not exactly overflowing with self-confidence. I think he's a little on the shy side; that he'd be more apt to make a move if he thought you might be a little receptive. Let's face it, Allison, nobody likes being rejected."

"You're telling *me*?"

Ms. Hartley came along, and we shelved it for the time being. "We hear you're giving us an exam," Susannah said, following her into the classroom.

"Sorry about that, girls, but the principal says my classes are 'too loosely structured'; that I have to tighten them up, whatever *that* means. I tried arguing, but he's the principal. Me, I'm only a lowly teacher."

"A super teacher," I amended, and Susannah said, "Right on!"

Ms. Hartley bowed and said, "My public!" She put a hand on Susannah's arm. "Listen, if you're having any problems with the work, feel free. You have my home number. Just give me a call. You can come over, and we'll go over it together, okay?"

"Oh, right. Sure, Ms. Hartley, I'll do that," Susannah said, beating a hasty retreat to her seat.

"Are you having problems with the English?" I said when we were driving home to my house after school. "If so, you ought to consider taking Ms. H. up on her offer."

"No sweat. I'll just ditch school that day. I'm due to come down with something anyway."

"Is this what you do when you're not prepared for a test? Ditch school?"

"I know, it's very delinquent of me, and I didn't use to, at least not 'til recently, but how long can a person keep beating herself over the head before she finally gets wise? If I'm going to flunk either way, why keep putting myself through all that tension and aggravation? Better to just skip it. I wind up with the same grade."

"Wonderful! But there must be some other way of dealing with the situation. Have you tried studying, for instance?"

"Forget it. Not for *me*. No matter how much studying I do, I still flunk. And Shakespeare, well, it might as well be another language, Greek, for instance."

She obviously didn't want to talk about it, so I let it be.

Up in my room, Susannah started getting her equipment together, pulling all these bottles and jars out of her makeup case, lining them all up on my dresser. I watched her, feeling a little uptight. When you're used to being one person, the idea of suddenly being transformed into another person can be threatening, especially if you have a sneaking suspicion you're going to wind up looking even worse than before.

"I look very silly in makeup," I said. Like a little kid playing grown-up."

"Not when *I* put it on you, you don't!"

"You actually use all that gunk?"

"Not all at once, no." She shook up a bottle of makeup base, looking at my face the way I imagine my mother looks at a scalp just before making that crucial first incision. Then she tipped the bottle onto her fingers and began dabbing makeup base on my cheeks, chin, forehead, and the tip of my non-nose. She blended it in. It felt weird, as though I had a mask on.

"What's that?" I asked, watching her rub some reddish-bronze goo in the palm of her hand.

"Just blusher. Don't clutch," she replied, dabbing some on each cheekbone, then smoothing it in. She applied some eyeshadow, three different shades — pinky beige, mushroom, and copper.

After the eyeshadow, came mascara, eyebrow pencil, and finally, lipstick.

"Okay, you can look," she said, dragging me over to the mirror. I must admit, it was a shock. I couldn't believe what I was seeing. Suddenly, I had cheekbones and a nose. My eyes were big and luminous, still peering out from behind glasses of course, but looking anything but pale and nondescript.

"Is that *me*?" I said in a small voice, staring at the unfamiliar-looking girl in the mirror.

"Well, it's not *me*. I'm the one with the long hair," she smiled.

"What happened to my chin?"

"It's still there. I made it look a little less, um . . ."

"Prominent?"

"Right! Do you like the way your eyes look?"

"Do I! Are you joshing? You know what, Susannah? You could do this for a living."

"Unfortunately, I probably will someday," she replied in a sarcastic tone.

"It's like magic."

"Not magic. I told you, it's just a matter of learning how, that's all."

"I couldn't do it. Not in a million years!"

"Allison, every female between the ages of twelve and ninety can. A lot of males these days, too. So why not *you*?"

"You'd be surprised what a klutz I can be when I'm uptight."

"Oh, come on, Allison! You don't have to be a genius to be able to put on makeup." She looked at me with this appraising expression. "We *must* do something with that hair! Now, with the make-up on and all, it looks pretty bedraggled."

"That's a nice way of putting it. More like the pits! But that's just it. The kind of hair I have, it just won't do anything. It just sits there."

"The guy who cuts my hair is a genius. He'll make it behave, believe me."

"You know," I said, contemplating her, "I really ought to start jogging . . ."

"Well, we will," she said, launching into this whole, long thing about how we were going to jog together every morning, starting the very next day. I felt like Eliza Doolittle in *My Fair Lady*, in the process of being transformed from an ugly duckling into a beautiful swan.

In the midst of my reverie, I heard Susannah saying, "I hope you know what you're going to do with him once you get him, because Beautiful Bobby Stern is practically yours, girl!"

We were in the kitchen, having a cup of tea, when my folks came in. My dad took one look at me and slumped against the door of the refrigerator, doing this comic imitation of someone fainting from shock. He didn't ever overreact from his first glimpse of the beauteous Susannah, he was so focused on overreacting to the new me.

"Daddy, honestly! It doesn't make that much of a difference," I said, blushing.

"If your own father doesn't recognize you, you can bet it does!" he replied, grinning happily at me.

My mother was looking at me as though she had never seen me before in her life. "What a difference a little makeup makes," she mused, her hand going to her face.

"A *little* makeup?" I laughed. "Like about fifty dollars' worth. Susannah used enough to stock an entire cosmetics department at Robinson's. Susannah thinks I ought to get a haircut. Do you think I ought to get a haircut, Mom?"

My mother glanced at Susannah, then back at me. Then she did something totally out of character for her — she ventured an opinion. "I think you ought to get a haircut, Allison," she said, and I thought I heard trumpets blowing. "Oh, I almost forgot," she added, making a face. "There's a board meeting at the hospital tomorrow, so Daddy and I won't be able to get away. I'm so terribly sorry, darling. Will you take a raincheck? We can do it some other time."

I shrugged, thinking she looked pathetically guilt-ridden, and said, "Oh, it's okay, Mom. Really. I guess now I've got something else to do anyway."

"Makeup, haircuts. What next?" my father said, looking a little threatened. "I hope you're not going to turn into another person. I like the person you *are*." He looked at my mother. "Are we going through the Andrea Syndrome again, Laura? I don't think I can take it!"

"I got an appointment for tomorrow," Susannah said when she had called her beauty parlor. "Chick's booked, but Dusty said he'll do it. Your parents are nice! I really like your father. He's funny. You know, when you think back, all I remember about my father is he yelled a lot. He never talked in a normal tone of voice. When he left, it was like there was something missing. I couldn't figure out why it got so quiet all of a sudden."

"What's your mom like?"

"Oh, a worrier. She worries about me a lot; about my future. She worries that I'll get into the wrong things, go out with the wrong boy, be poor, have to struggle, wind up a waitress, or a file clerk, like her. She worries that I'll flunk out of high school, because that'll mean I won't have any future, and to her, that's the worst thing in the world, not to have a future. To me, too, I guess, but what can I do? I can't have a brain transplant, and short of that nothing's going to help."

"Your grades are that bad?"

"Worse! Listen, half the time I don't even know what's going on in class. You don't know how that feels, sitting there, knowing everyone understands but you; that you're the only one in the room who's totally out of it. Before an exam, I get sick, throw up and everything, I get so nervous. Finally, out of desperation, I started ditching school on exam days. I figured, if I didn't do *something*, I'd wind up with ulcers or something."

"Would it help if you got a tutor?"

She shook her head. "I've been that route, and it didn't make any difference. It's hard for a person like you to understand," she said in a small voice, not looking at me. "School's such a breeze for you, you'd get straight A's if you never showed up. But I could sit with my nose in a book from now 'til Doomsday, and it wouldn't matter. I'd still be dumb. There's one basic difference between you and me, Allison. Your problem you can *do* something about. Mine, I can't. You want to improve your looks, right? That's easy. Looks you can do something about improving. But brains? No way! You've got 'em or you haven't, and that's all there is to it."

"I don't agree with you," I argued. "It looks to me as though what we've got here is a case of a massive inferiority complex at work, working overtime. You *think* you're dumb, so when the chips are down, and you're faced with a test or an assignment, you can't perform. It's like a mental block. Your tremendous lack of confidence keeps you from fulfilling your basic intellectual potential."

"I haven't *got* a basic intellectual potential," she said, starting to get angry.

—— 7 ——

Next day Susannah took me to her beauty parlor, this hole in the wall in Sherman Oaks called His & Hers, Unlimited, owned by these two guys, Dusty and Chick. Dusty and Chick were ex-actors who, when they found out they couldn't make it in the movies, decided to open their own beauty parlor instead. Chick's wife was the manicurist, and Dusty's girlfriend Tamara was the receptionist.

"This is where you come to get your hair done?" I whispered to Susannah. Chick must have heard me, because he gave me this vicious look and said to Susannah, "What did you bring me? Next time, don't do me any favors!" As you can imagine, this got us off to a great start.

Luckily, or unluckily, depending on how you looked at it, my appointment was with Dusty, not Chick. From the haircut he gave the girl before me, I thought maybe I ought to hop the first bus home. I sat there in the chair, water dripping down my nose, listening to Susannah and Dusty discussing what he ought to do with me, my ego slowly shriveling to the size of a pea as they went down this whole, long list of all my many short-comings and less-than-favorable physical attributes. Finally, Dusty grabbed a pair of scissors and starting snipping away, flourishing the scissors in the air between each snip, like a concert pianist playing Beethoven.

"He's very creative," Susannah said, smiling reassuringly at me. I tried not to clutch, but there was an awful lot of hair all over the plastic cape I had on, all over the floor all around us, but little left on my head.

"A crew cut?" I squeaked, staring at myself in the mirror. "That's what you dragged me all the way to Sherman Oaks for, *a crew cut*?"

"Allison, it's going to look super!" Susannah gushed, smiling at Dusty.

"Super for whom? Susannah, I wanted a hair-cut, not to be *bald*!"

"If she says another word, I'll hand her over to Chick." Dusty glared at me in the mirror. From the way he said it, obviously being handed over to Chick was a fate worse than death.

I glared back. "Stop being temperamental. You're not the one who has to walk out of here bald."

"She's a little nervous," Susannah said to Dusty in a placating tone.

"Yeah, who isn't? It's called the Gamin Cut,"

Dusty said to me. "Didn't you know? Short hair's back in style."

"Short? This isn't short. If it was just short, I could live with it."

My hair was about an eighth of an inch long all over, except at the back of my neck where it was long and scraggly. Dusty had cut it sharply around my ears, so they stuck out even more than normal, and that was particularly upsetting to me, because I had always had a complex about my ears, among other things. At the top of my head, some of the hair was cut so short, it stood up like a crew cut.

"Didn't you notice I have stickout ears?" I said to Dusty.

"Of course I noticed. I'm not blind," he replied, giving me a haughty look. "What have ears got to do with your hairstyle? You wouldn't want to walk around wearing the wrong hairstyle, one that's not right for your face, just because you wanted to cover your ears, would you? Think of it this way. Would Barbara Streisand comb her hair down over her nose?"

"Ears aren't noses," I muttered, glaring up at him. "They happen to be situated in a much more convenient spot for covering up."

He and I went on sparring back and forth that way for a while. By the time we left, I was beginning to feel a little better about the hair, and he was beginning to feel a little better about *me*.

"Your friend's real clever," he said to Susannah. "Cute, too."

"You're upset, aren't you?" Susannah said when we were driving home to my house.

"Oh, no! What makes you think that? If anyone I know sees me, I'll just kill myself, that's all."

Aside from investing in a wig, or keeping a hat on twenty-four hours a day, my only alternative was to lock myself in my room for a month or two until it grew back. When we pulled into my driveway, I looked around to make sure none of my neighbors was around before running out of the car and making a beeline for the front door.

"Hiya, Al," a voice said. I froze in my tracks. Sitting with his feet on my mother's favorite pot of geraniums was Bobby. "What happened to you?" he said, staring at my hair.

"Dusty is what happened to me, and you better hope he never happens to you!" I muttered, fumbling for my house key.

"I like it. It's kind of cute," he said, smiling at me. "What did you do to your face? It looks different."

"I'm wearing makeup, dummy," I hissed, struggling with the lock.

"How come you never wore it before?"

"I did. I do. Just not to school."

He followed me inside, Susannah hard on his heels. "You look nifty, Al," he said. "I really like it, the hair *and* the face."

"Who wouldn't?" Susannah said, grinning at me.

"I thought you went whale-watching," I said to Bobby.

"I'm going now. Just came over to say goodbye."

"You're only going for the day, right?"

"Right. But what if something happened to me,

if the boat got sunk or something, and we never saw each other again? You'd want to have said one last good-bye, wouldn't you?"

I headed for the kitchen, totally nonplussed.

Helga saw me and let out a shriek. "What happened to you? Does your mother know?"

"Helga, I'm sixteen. Every time I'm going to get a haircut, I don't go running to my mommy to ask her permission."

"Oh, really? When was the last time you got a haircut, nineteen-seventy-one?"

Susannah, Bobby, and I sat out back, drinking iced tea. Susannah and Bobby talked about whales and dolphins. I sat there concentrating on becoming invisible. I thought he'd never leave.

"What was he doing here anyway?" I said when he was gone.

Susannah gave me this incredulous look and said, "Take a wild guess! Look, Cinderella, let's go and get you some clothes, huh? Now that we've gotten this far, it's a definite must!"

We drove to the Promenade. I kept thinking everybody was staring at me. Susannah kept saying it was all in my imagination, but I swear, they were. The prices of the clothes in the stores were really outrageous.

"Now you know why I design and make all my own clothes." Susannah said, checking out a T-shirt dress.

"All those unreal things you wear, you make them yourself?" I said.

She held up a shirt for my inspection, a long, man-tailored one with pinstripes and a tab collar.

"I can't afford to buy stuff that's ready-made. Besides, who wants to walk around looking like everyone else? I like to look unique, have a look of my own. I have expensive taste. I know the difference between good stuff and junk, no matter what the price tag might say. I'd never be able to afford the kind of clothes I'd want to buy in a million years."

"I'm duly impressed," I said, checking out a pair of baggy trousers. "You keep talking about how you have no future. You could be a fashion designer. You've got the talent. If Mrs. Stern can do it, you definitely could! I bet she doesn't design and make all her own clothes."

"Just what the fashion world is waiting for, *me!*" Susannah said, taking a light gray cotton cableknit sweater off a rack. It had short sleeves, a little lace collar, and a narrow, black silk bow tie. "Allison," she said, "a girl who can't even graduate from high school is going to have a bit of a problem getting into design school. Even if I do have the talent, what difference will it make if I can't hack the work?"

She spotted a rack of things on sale and took off like a shot, rifling through all this stuff that looked like just a bunch of rags to me. For the next hour and a half she dashed in and out of the dressing room, bringing me all this stuff to try on, aided and abetted by a salesperson who turned out to be the head ladies' sportswear buyer of the whole store and who, I have no doubt, was taking notes. Most of the stuff I would never have dreamed of choosing for myself, but as Susannah kept reminding me, I didn't know diddley about style anyway. I have to admit, each time I would voice my disapproval, thinking the thing would look horrendous on me, I'd put it on, and it would look great, which proved Susannah really *did* know about style, and I knew diddley.

"I just wish I didn't have these fat thighs," I kept saying, looking at myself in the mirror.

"Don't worry. You start jogging, and no more thighs!"

I wound up buying two pairs of baggies, the charcoal-gray and a red pair, two shirts, a vest, a gray cableknit sweater, a jeans skirt (would you believe purple?), and a suit Susannah found stashed away on a rack on sale, what she called an "unstructured" jacket with matching trousers in kind of a muted mauvish-gray and cream color stripe.

"This is my new look, huh?" I said, watching the saleslady, who was really a buyer, add up the bill, holding my breath because I just knew it was exorbitant.

"Right! Your new look, classic, understated, but definitely stylish. Kind of *Early Ingenue*."

"Looks more like *Early Boyish* to me."

The saleslady looked at me and smiled. "Just stick with your friend, dear. She knows exactly what she's doing!"

We went to The Shoe Conspiracy, and I got these wild shoes, a pair of violet colored leather, low-heeled sandals, and another pair, flat fisherman's sandals in a kind of loden green. Susannah wanted me to buy cowboy boots on sale, but I balked.

"Enough is enough! I'm already hysterical about all the money I spent. My mother will kill me!"

"But she said you needed clothes."

"Yes, but everything in the store?"

We went to Robinson's to get me some underwear to replace the rags I'd been wearing, and some makeup so I wouldn't have to keep borrowing Susannah's.

Susannah picked up the packages and said, "I'm dying of thirst, aren't you? Let's have an Orange Julius. They're loaded with calories, but we'll share one."

"You know," I said to her when we were at the Orange Julius counter, "I've been giving a lot of thought to the problem with your grades, and I think I've come up with a solution; sort of a reciprocal trade agreement, a mutual pact between the two of us, whereby *you* help *me* improve my looks, *I* help *you* improve your grades. I have a feeling, if we studied together, it would help you pull your grades up."

She took a sip of the drink, then handed it to me. "You're a doll to offer, but it wouldn't work. Like I said, you've got it or you don't, and I don't. Being smart isn't contagious. It wouldn't rub off."

"Stop saying that, Susannah! See, that's your whole problem. You *think* you're dumb."

I started doing this whole, long bit, trying to convince her to give it a try. All of a sudden this cute guy came over. He stood there contemplating the menu, looking confused. Finally he said,

"Ladies, what do you recommend, the orange, the pineapple, or the strawberry?"

"Huh?" I said, my usual socially with-it self

"I prefer the orange myself," Susannah drawled, giving him this long, slow, appraising look, making it pretty obvious she liked what she saw. "My friend here likes pineapple, but of course if strawberry's your thing . . ."

"Three large orange," the guy said to the kid behind the counter.

"You're going to drink *three*?" I asked.

"No, one's for me, the other two are for my friends over there," he replied, beckoning to these other two guys, one kind of drippy; one real cute, a cowboy type, complete with long blond hair, Buffalo Bill moustache, cowboy hat, cowboy boots, Levi's, the whole California look. I would have bet money on his owning a pickup truck with at least three dogs in the back.

"I'm Scott," the first guy said, looking at Susannah. "This is Danny, and the one in the cowboy suit, that's Mitch. Say hello to the nice girls, guys."

Everyone introduced themselves. I stood there trying to act debonair, as though this sort of thing happened in my life every day. Susannah handled the situation with casual aplomb, but why wouldn't she? For *her* this *was* an everyday occurrence. How did she manage to come up with just the right things to say at the drop of a hat like that? A person who was dumb couldn't do that. She communicated, very subtly, of course, that if they were real, real nice, we might condescend to see them sometime again. Not *would*, you understand, just *might*, if they played their cards right, as my dad would have said. It was all a relevation to me, an area of expertise I was sure I'd never be able to master.

They told us they went to Cal State Northridge, this college nearby, and asked where we went to school. Without even thinking I blurted, "Leland High!"

"Why'd you tell them that?" Susannah said when we were heading for the parking lot.

"You mean I shouldn't have?"

She raised her eyes and muttered to herself. Then, "Look, promise me something. Next time we run into three cute guys, shut up and let me do the talking, okay?"

When I got home, my parents weren't there, which was probably just as well under the circumstances. By the time my mom saw my hair, it was the following day. I came down for breakfast just as she was dashing out the door. When she saw me, she stopped and stood there staring at me.

"Allison, your hair!"

"I know. Don't say it, Mom. It'll only make me feel worse."

"Say what?" she asked, transfixed with shock.

"That you don't like it. What else?"

"Do you like it?" she said, right in character. I shook my head, and she asked, "Why not?"

"Why not? Mom, look at my ears. And my chin. Mom, I look like a *boy*, a boy with stickout ears."

"Do you really think so? I was just going to say

how pert and feminine you look. What's wrong with your ears?" she said, getting defensive all of a sudden. "There's nothing wrong with your ears!"

"You only say that because they're just like yours!"

"I say it because there's nothing wrong with your ears!" She glanced at her watch. "I have to run. By the way, Helga says you bought some nice new clothes. Maybe tonight you'll give me a fashion show."

"A fashion show? Really, Mom!"

"Oh, I forgot, tonight's the fund-raising committee meeting. We'll make it tomorrow, for sure!"

— 8 —

Next morning, at the crack of dawn, Susannah showed up at the front door, all togged out for jogging. I was still half-asleep. She made me go upstairs and get dressed, and the two of us took off into the sunrise. She jogged. I sort of shlumped along after her, totally wiped out after the first block.

"If people were supposed to perambulate this rapidly, they'd all be born with roller skates on," I grouched, dragging along behind her up Magnolia Hill.

Susannah said, "Just shut up and jog!"

It was a nice day, not smoggy or anything, and if you were a nature freak, which I'm not, you probably would have been in heaven, jogging into the hills, listening to the birdies chirping, watching the flowers grow. I thought I was dying. Susannah said I wasn't, but that I would if I didn't remember to breathe. I tried, but every time I filled my lungs, I got so dizzy, I nearly passed out.

We were coming up Magnolia Hill when we saw this person jogging toward us. I could tell it was a person, but that's about it, since I didn't have my glasses on. Susannah gave me a massive nudge, nearly knocking me flat, and whispered, "What a boy!" As the person jogged passed me, I got a fleeting impression of a lot of strawberry blond curls, dazzling white teeth flashing a grin, and an expanse of copper-tanned skin. "Oh, what a boy!" Susannah said again. "Who is he anyway?"

A little while later, we were jogging back down Magnolia, and there he was, getting into this snazzy red Mercedes 250 SL convertible.

"Quick! Get the license number," I said to Susannah, making a joke. "That way you'll be able to track him down."

"Darn! Too late," she muttered in all seriousness as the Mercedes disappeared around the corner. My legs were threatening to go on strike, but Susannah insisted I jog all the way back to my house without stopping once. I collapsed in the doorway, pretending to have died. She hauled me to my feet, giving me this whole number about how I must be in some terrible shape if a little jogging could wipe me out like that.

"A little jogging?" I squawked. "We just jogged at least five miles."

"Make it two," she said, giving me a look. "I clocked it."

We showered and got dressed, then had breakfast — fresh orange juice, melon with cottage cheese, one slice of whole grain toast each, dry, no margarine or butter (yuk!), and herbal tea. While we were eating, Susannah did an ecstatic monologue about the boy in the red 250 SL, berating herself for not having done something drastic in order to get his attention, worrying herself sick over whether she would ever see him again in her lifetime. It was late. I kept dropping subtle hints, glancing at my watch, but she went on and on, until finally I just said, "Hey, shut up and help me clean up. We're about to be late for homeroom!"

When we got to school, she had to practically carry me up the stairs, my legs were so totally ruined and useless. "You come into my life, and the next thing you know, I'm a cripple," I muttered, limping in through the main entrance.

The new me turned out to be the main topic of conversation all day; in fact, all week. I don't think anybody in the whole school talked about anything else. The way they carried on, I got the impression they thought it was a vast improvement, bordering on the miraculous.

"I sure must have been ugly," I said to Susannah.

"Well," she said, smiling at me, "if you were, you're not anymore. You know that old saying, 'You are what you wear'? Enough said!"

"Not 'You are what you wear,' Susannah. 'You are what you eat.'"

"Are you sure? I thought it was 'You are what you wear.'"

"Listen, take it from me, daughter of the Cliché King. It's eat, not wear."

Bobby got to school late. "What happened? Did you stay out all night whale-watching?" I asked.

"No, I was up all night. Timmy got sick, woke up at three A.M. again."

During lunch, Susannah, Bobby, and I were sitting together. Marshall came over and said, "Hey, guys, I'm not going to be able to be here the day of the report. My folks are going to Lake Tahoe to ski for a week and they want me to go with them."

"Terrific!" Susannah said, looking at me.

Marshall said, "Hey, what do you want me to do? It's not my fault my folks are going skiing."

"What can you do. It's your parents," I put in, smiling up at Marshall, controlling the impulse to dump my yogurt over his head.

"Gee, that's tough, Marshall," Susannah said, offering him a bite of her apple.

"But those are the breaks, pal," Bobby went on, looking at me. "Look, just go ahead. Have a ball. We'll just have to manage without you. Of course, since you're not going to be doing any of the work on this project, you won't expect us to share our grade with you. That really would be unfair."

"Aw, come on," Marshall said, handing Susannah back her apple. "I can't afford to fail. Coach Jameson'll boot me off the team."

"That's the way it goes," I sighed, shaking my head.

"What's fair is fair," said Susannah, taking a bite of her apple.

"The team'll just have to carry on without you, Marshall, old sport!" Bobby put in.

"Okay, okay, cool it already. I got the message," Marshall muttered, glaring at us. "I'll tell my folks I can't go. A week skiing at Tahoe, and I have to pass it up on account of a dumb, stupid social science project!"

"Do you believe this guy?" I muttered to Bobby when Marshall flexed away down the hall. "He's annoyed at us for spoiling his ski week."

I was heading for my next class, when I ran into Trisha, who gave me one of her usual snippy smirks. "You and Miss Teenage America are getting pretty chummy. Is that why you're doing all these things to yourself? Getting your hair cut, putting on makeup every day, buying new clothes and all? Because you want to look like your new girlfriend?"

"That'd be a good trick, wouldn't it, Trisha?" I said, and started to walk away.

"Maybe Susannah'll get you some dates with boys," Trisha persisted, coming after me. "If you're real, real nice to her, maybe she'll throw a few of her rejects your way. Bobby Stern maybe, if you're real lucky."

Later, when I was leaving school, Bobby came running after me. "Need a lift home?"

"Sure. Great! I was dreading the bus," I said, following him to the car. "You know, sometimes it's a drag, living by your principles," I confided, sliding in beside him. "Sometimes I think it'd be a lot easier just to go along; you know, flow with things, not make waves like I do."

73

He shot me a look. "Wrong!" he said, shaking his head emphatically. "If you don't stick up for what you believe in, and stay true to who you really are, you lose respect for yourself, and other people lose respect for you, too. People like you and I, we're the rare ones. That's the reason the world's in such a mess."

"Thanks! I needed that," I sighed. "Sometimes it just seems like such a hassle, it's almost not worth it, but I guess it is. I wouldn't want to be like everybody else anyway. That'd be boring."

He pulled the car out of the parking lot. Heading down Oak Drive, I felt him looking at me and turned with a smile. "What're you looking at?"

"You."

"Oh! Better keep your eyes on the road. Watch out. There's a stop sign."

"Listen, you want to drive? No, I didn't think so. So, don't be a backseat driver, okay? You know, you sure look different with makeup and that new hairdo," he added, dazzling me with his smile. "I really like you with short hair."

"You do? I really clutched at first, but I'm getting used to it. It's sure a cinch to take care of. You just shampoo it, run your fingers through it a few times, and that's it. A no-hassle hairstyle."

"Did you pass your driver's test yet?" he asked, changing the subject. "I'll take you out for some practice sessions if you like."

"That'd be super." I shot him a smile. "I think that's half the reason I failed, because I never got a chance to practice. My parents are never around to take me out."

"Yeah, mine, too. That's why my brother came in handy. If Andrea were around, you could ask her to take you."

The rest of the way home, all he talked about were his beloved whales. I remember saying, in an offhand way, that I wouldn't mind going whale-watching sometime; that I thought it was probably fascinating. That's when he said, "Look, there's another expedition in a few weeks. Want to go with me on this one?"

I said something sarcastic; something like, "You mean you'd actually take a female whale-watching with you?"

He said, "Lots of females go whale-watching, dopey. This friend of mine, Judy, goes practically every week. She's really into whales."

"Judy? Who's Judy?"

"This friend of mine. She's into oceanography and marine biology, too." He started telling me all about wonderful Judy, making her sound like the world's most sensational girl. To say I was a trifle jealous would be the understatement of the century, but I think I covered it up.

"Thanks for the lift," I said when we pulled into my driveway, mentally adding, *And give my regards to Judy!*

"Hey," he said, grinning at me, "you doing anything this weekend? Because there's a great double feature at the Valley Cinema, two horror flicks, oldies but goodies. Want to go?"

"With *you*?"

"No, with my dad."

"This weekend?"

"Yeah. Saturday night."

The way he had asked me, so casually, as though he was inquiring about a Math assignment or something, kind of confused me. This wasn't the way it was supposed to happen at all. I had been fantasizing about this moment for such a long time, and in my fantasies he always got down on one knee, or swept me into his arms and kissed me passionately first before asking me to go out with him.

"Are you with me, Al?" he said, snapping his fingers under my nose.

"Um, sure. Are you talking about Saturday night?"

"Yeah, Saturday night."

"Oh, um, yeah. I can make it."

He pulled out of the driveway, and I went inside, very cool, calm, and collected. The minute the door shut behind me, I let out a whoop and yelled, "HE ASKED ME OUT!"

Helga came rushing from the kitchen. "What happened. What's wrong? Are you all right, Allison?"

"Sure, I'm all right. Don't I look all right? I'm so incredibly all right, it's unbelievable! He actually asked me out," I said, throwing my books in the air.

She gave them a disapproving look, then looked at me and said, "*Who* asked you out?"

"Guess!"

"I don't know. You tell me."

"Okay, I will. None other than Bobby Stern!"

"Oh," she shrugged, turning around and heading back to the kitchen. "Is *that* all? The way you

76

were carrying on, I thought maybe it was Robert Redford."

When I called Susannah, she said, "See? What did I tell you? It's just a matter of getting your message across. Listen, what're you wearing Saturday night?"

"I don't know. You're the fashion expert. You tell me."

"How about the gray pants and the light gray sweater? If only you had bought those cowboy boots that were on sale at The Shoe Conspiracy. They'd be perfect."

"Why can't I wear the violet clunkers? Aren't they okay?"

"I guess, but the boots would've been better."

"Hey, the other phone's ringing. I'll call you back," I said and made a mad dash for the den. It was my mother, calling to tell me she and Daddy were coming home and wanted to take me out to dinner.

"Daddy says he wants to show off his beautiful daughter," she said, and I heard my father in the background saying, "Laura, I didn't say that!"

I was sort of surprised. Not that going out to dinner was such a rare occurrence in our family. When you've got parents who both work, you get to do it all the time, but it was a school day tomorrow, and my folks didn't usually like to take me out on a school night.

We went to The Pickwick Papers, this English-type pub where they serve the best roast beef and have the neatest salad bar in the Valley, one about forty feet long with every kind of raw vegetable imaginable, plus all these extras: sesame seeds, garbanzo beans, pickled beets, bacon bits, and grated Parmesan cheese. You could make a meal just going back for seconds, thirds, and fourths on salad.

"Isn't that Lou and Myra over there?" my father said when the hostess showed us to our seats, waving at a couple sitting across the room.

"I was hoping we wouldn't run into anyone we know," my mother grumbled, making a point of sitting on the side of the booth where her back would be to the couple, both of whom were smiling away, waving up a storm. "I'm just so tired," Mom said, slumping in her seat. "If I have to smile and make nice to one more person, I will definitely scream!"

"Have a glass of wine. You'll feel better," I said, looking over the menu. Not that you really had that much of a choice. It was roast beef or roast beef.

"You look adorable in that vest, Allison," my mother said.

"I don't want to look adorable. I want to look sexy," I countered, staring at my plate.

"That, too," she said airily, and I muttered, "Sure!"

"Well, that young man at that table over there seems to think so," she said and giggled.

My head shot up. "What young man?" I hissed, feeling my face begin to burn at the mere suggestion that I was the object of anyone's scrutiny. Across the room, alone at a table in the corner, this cute guy was staring at me. When he saw me looking, he smiled, and I dropped my eyes, my face burning. My parents thought it was precious,

78

also humorous. I was so humiliated, I wanted to crawl under the table and finish my dinner there.

"I should have had a tunafish sandwich at home," I said to Susannah when I called her later. "By the way, I meant to tell you, I spoke to Ms. Hartley about us studying together, and she thinks it's a super idea. She said we ought to work on all our courses together, that it would be good for both of us. Not just you. Me, too."

"I don't know," Susannah hedged. "I just don't think it'll do any good, that's all."

"Well, we can give it a try, can't we? If it works, great. If not, well, at least we can say we explored all the possibilities."

"What're you wearing to the school concert next Saturday night?" Susannah asked, conveniently changing the subject. "I heard everyone in the school orchestra's going formal."

"Uh, everyone but me," I said, thinking that designer jeans would be about as formal as I'd ever want to get. "I have this dress I got for my cousin's wedding last year," I offered, wondering if it still fit. "I could wear that, I guess."

"If I know you, it's a doozy," Susannah laughed. "I could make you something, you know, something smashing. A soloist in a school concert ought to have something wonderful to wear to the big concert."

"Make me something? You're not serious, are you?"

"Of course I am. Look, have you forgotten who I am, that super duper fashion designer, Susannah Ellis. Not only am I talented, I'm also speedy. Tomorrow after school we'll go to Sew 'n Sew and pick out some fabric. By the day after tomorrow, you'll have a dress for the concert."

"Uh-uh," I replied, wondering if she was purposely copping out, or if she had forgotten. "Tomorrow we're going to study, remember?"

"Oh, sure. Study. We'll do that, too. There's plenty of time to do both. Hey, I really *want* to do this, Allison, so let me, okay?"

At lunch in the cafeteria next day, Bobby said to me, "Why don't we go out to dinner before the movie Saturday night? Have you ever eaten at El Torito? It's pretty good. Or I know this great Chinese restaurant in Chatsworth, Hunan Garden. We could go there. Unless you like Italian food, in which case . . ."

"I'm crazy for Chinese food," I ventured, surreptitiously pinching myself to see whether I was dreaming.

"Great! So am I," he said. "I'll pick you up around seven."

"I dreamt that, right?" I whispered to Susannah when he had taken off down the hall.

"If so, so did I," she whispered back. "Love in bloom!" she exclaimed, taking off down the corridor, flapping her wings and chirping like a birdie. Everyone stared at her, because this was not exactly Susannah Ellis's style. Doing something so cuckoo, and so spontaneous, was out of character for the girl who always walked around so aloof and reserved.

"Susannah, just because a boy asks a girl to have something to eat and see a movie, that doesn't mean he's madly in love with her, especially if that boy and that girl happen to know each other going on eleven years and are friends!"

"Oh, really? Right! He just needed company and the guys were all busy, that's all," she said.

"How do you feel about mauve?" she said to me when we were at Sew 'n Sew after school, checking out fabric until I was so confused, I couldn't tell navy-blue from shocking pink.

"How does mauve feel about me?" I muttered, eyeing the exit. "Could we go home? I'm getting an atrocious headache. You don't know how much I hate shopping, Susannah."

"That's okay. I love it enough for the both of us," she said, pulling me away from this houndstooth check I was looking at. "You're sixteen, remember? Look at this mauve silk. It would make up beautifully. Know how I see it?"

"No. How?"

"As an Edwardian-style dress, you know, with a high neck with a little lace ruff, lace-trimmed pintucking on the bodice, long sleeves — muttonchop maybe — with lace on the cuffs, a full skirt with a wide sash. All you'd need is a picture hat and white gloves, and you'd be set for a garden party with the queen at Buckingham Palace."

"But would I be all set for a concert at Leland High?" I said, looking at the mauve silk as though I thought it was going to bite me. "Susannah, I'll look like a tub-and-a-half in a mauve silk Edwardian dress for a garden party, and you know it!"

"No, you won't. Allison, don't you know *any-thing* about style? Wearing sweatshirts as big as tents is not the way to make yourself look slimmer. Other than dieting, exercising, and losing weight, dressing properly can do the trick. But dressing properly, that's something you know absolutely zilch, zero, *nada*, about!"

"I have the feeling I'm going to learn though," I said, watching her pick up the bolt of fabric and lug it up to the cashier. "Lace pintucking? Ruffles? Sashes? Aren't those slightly frilly and fussy for a girl who's new look is supposed to be Early Ingenue?" I couldn't help saying.

"Early Ingenue's your daytime look, silly. Your nighttime look, that's something else again. Besides, you're not just *going* to that concert. You're playing a solo in it. Look, trust me, okay?"

"I don't want you to think I'm being negative," she said to me when we were driving home to my house, "but you have no idea what a colossal dud I am when it comes to Shakespeare. I hate the stuff and I don't understand any of it."

I looked at her and laughed. "Look, just leave it to me. By the time I get through with you, you're going to be an expert."

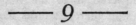

— 9 —

Those certainly were famous last words!

I hadn't reckoned on the enormity of Susannah's mental block, her complete and total lack of even the most rudimentary study habits, her almost superhuman lack of confidence.

You know how teachers are always alluding to those things called study habits, putting such an emphasis on our developing good ones? Well, I'd never really given much thought to study habits, mainly because I'd been born with mine. They just came with the territory, built in, so I'd never had to work at developing any, or to consider how other people did, or didn't.

In Susannah's case, not only did she lack study habits, but she was totally lacking in concentration, too. She couldn't, really couldn't, concentrate for more than sixty seconds running.

"*This* is how you study?" I said, watching her

do leg lifts while lying on her back on the floor in my room, the book of Shakespeare's plays propped up on her belly. "Susannah, if you want to learn this, you have to concentrate, and you can't concentrate doing six other things at the same time."

"Yes, I can. I *am* concentrating." She lifted her left leg in the air, held it to the count of sixty, then lowered it to the floor. "What is it about this stuff that just turns me off? It's so boring! I mean, the language, it's so old-fashioned. Why would anybody want to read it anyway? This guy Shakespeare has been dead for hundreds of years."

"Susannah, *he* may be, but his plays are still very much alive and kicking. Anyway, there's nothing old-fashioned about old Will. His people are so real, they could easily be living today. Just the language, and the way they dress, are old-fashioned. The way they act isn't. Look, if it would help any, we could update it. You know, get rid of the flowery language. Think of it as a modern play, one that was written by someone who's alive today. You understand the story, don't you?"

"How could I? I can't read it!"

"Well, I'll give you a quick synopsis, okay?"

I started filling her in on the story, getting really excited, because I'd come up with such a miraculous brainstorm, thinking if this approach didn't work, nothing would.

"See, there are these two girls, cousins, Rosalind and Celia. They're not only cousins, they're best friends. Anyway, Rosalind's father is Celia's dad's brother, and vice versa, but they don't get along at all. In fact, only recently Celia's dad booted Roz's right out of the country, banished him to live in this forest without even a roof over his head. Celia talked her father into taking Roz in, since poor Roz had nowhere else to go, and now Roz is living in Celia's father's house. From here on in, it's a lot less complicated. Okay, so Celia's old man, he's pretty nasty. He's got a vicious temper. You look at him crooked, and he has you beheaded or something equally distasteful. So, of course, being the outspoken girl she is, Roz does something to rile him up, and he decides to boot her out, too. Celia decides to leave with her by dark of night, and the two of them slink away, heading for the forest to look for Roz's dear old dad. Only, since they're traveling alone and unprotected, Roz dresses up like a boy, and they pretend they're sister and brother. That way, they figure, they won't run into any trouble with all those weirdos and perverts who hang out in that forest."

I paused, looking over at her to see if she was tuning in or not. "Why'd you stop?" she said, sitting up. "Go on. It's a pretty good story."

"Okay, now take this scene here, in Act One, when Celia says she's going along, and Roz doesn't want her to. Don't let all the fancy words fool you. Forget all those *thou's* and *thee's*, *prithee's*, *pray tell's*, *whither goest thou's*, and *methinkses*. What's Celia actually saying? Just 'Hey, Coz, we're best friends, aren't we? How could you think I'd let you go off into that crazy forest alone? I'm going with you!' "

"That's all she's saying?' Susannah said, staring at the page as though it were written in Sanskrit.

"And this song,' I said, turning the page. "The one about the greenwood tree? Well, I mean, it's a little hard to relate to some guy who's singing about a greenwood tree in this day and age, right? So, just scratch that greenwood tree and pretend he's singing something by Bob Seger, Led Zeppelin, or The Beatles instead."

Susannah laughed delightedly and said, "You know, I might just wind up understanding this stuff after all!" She got up, came over to me, sat down next to me on the bed, and said, "Hey, friend, you're the greatest! Now, tell me what happens when Roz and Celia get to the forest. Do they find Roz's dear old dad? Or do they run into a couple of cute guys instead?"

Talk about insight! I mean, could someone dumb have tuned in so totally to what that play was all about? Definitely not. "You're going to be okay," I said, giving her a bop on the head. "There is definitely someone at home up there. Once you let her out, you're going to be in for a few major surprises!"

Next morning Susannah and I were jogging along together, when who do we see but The Boy, jogging down Magnolia Hill toward us. "Hi!" he said when he passed us, flashing this dazzler of a smile. The sun glinting off his whiter-than-white toothpaste-ad teeth nearly blinded me. I thought maybe he'd stop and chat, but no! That was it, the whole bit. Just "Hi," the smile, and off he went without a break in his rhythm.

"Why didn't he stop?" Susannah wailed, watching him go.

"He couldn't. Not allowed. When you're Super Jogger, you jog, not chase girls."

"He's gorgeous, I may die!" she said. "Allison, isn't he *gorgeous*?"

"Gorgeous. Just gorgeous!" Actually, he was, in a showy sort of way. Not my type in the least. You could tell, from one look at him, how vain and self-centered he was.

Next day was C.L. Day, which, loosely translated, means the day I got my contact lenses. I had to miss the first two periods of school because Dr. Koenig didn't make appointments after three P.M.

"He probably plays golf every day," I said to my mother when we were driving over to his office.

"No, tennis," she said with a perfectly straight face. Honestly, sometimes my particular brand of humor is totally wasted on my mom.

Dr. Koenig stuck me in this chair with all these gadgets attached to it and gave me the eye examination to end all eye examinations. It took an hour and a half, all told. Then he got out these miniscule slivers of clear plastic that looked like the punched-out holes from a plastic report cover and put them in my eyes. Let me tell you, while he was putting them in, I was working hard at not passing out. The idea of anybody putting anything in my eye, even something as miniscule as those lenses, made my stomach roll over and play dead.

"Now you try putting them in yourself," he said, rinsing them in a little vial of saline solution, stirring them around with a pair of tweezers, then dipping his finger into the vial and coming up with one. It sat there on the tip of his forefinger, glimmering at me, and I thought, *Is he kidding? I'll never get that thing in!* He held up the mirror and told me to tuck my chin and look straight upwards, then *zap* the little thing in, real sneaky-like, while I wasn't looking. I thought, *No way would that ever happen.* Figuring I'd better make out like I was at least trying, I touched my finger tip with the lens on it to my eyeball.

"If at first you don't succeed, try, try again, as my father would say," I muttered, blinking away. "Sorry, I goofed," I said to Dr. Koenig. "Now where is the little thing? Don't tell me I lost it already!"

"It's in your eye," Dr. Koenig said. "How does it feel? Not so bad, huh? Want to try the other one now? It's better if you can see out of both eyes, you know."

For the next few hours, I walked around seeing everything in six dimensions at least, bumping into things right and left all over the place, turning on everybody at school by winking and blinking at them. They must have thought I was really weird.

"I've got my new lenses in," I said to Susannah when we were walking to fifth period. "How do I look?"

"The same as when you're not wearing glasses, dopey," she laughed. "How do they feel? Do they feel strange?"

"Uh-uh. I just keep thinking I've got something in my eye, and everything looks a little rounder than before. I should have gotten colored ones, huh? Blue maybe. I always wanted blue eyes."

88

"Really? Why? Green is so much more interesting. Everybody and his brother have blue eyes."

Marshall came sauntering along, doing his Burt Reynolds imitation.

"Watch out! Here comes Mr. Macho. So, what's shaking, baby?" Susannah asked Marshall. "How many women have you swept off their feet *this* week?"

"Quite a few," Marshall said, looking mildly affronted. "Listen, you guys, I want to apologize. I guess that was really pushing it, going skiing with the report coming up. When I thought about it, I realized it was a crummy thing to do to the rest of you guys. I'm sorry."

"Hey, it's okay," I stammered, staring at him in disbelief, wondering if this really was Marshall. "Everybody's entitled to make a mistake once in a while, even you."

Bobby came along, looking beautiful. He walked over to me, slipped an arm around my waist, and said, "Hey, I missed you!"

"You just saw her yesterday," Susannah said, looking at me.

"Yeah, but that was twenty-four hours ago," Bobby said with a grin.

"If you had any doubts, I guess they're all cleared up now," she said to me when we were leaving school later. "If he made it any more obvious, he'd be walking around wearing a big flashing neon sign: BOBBY LOVES ALLISON!"

We went to her house so she could work on the dress. Her house wasn't anything like I'd expected. I guess I had just taken it for granted Susannah lived the same way I, and everyone else

I knew, did, in a pretty nice house, in a pretty nice neighborhood; you know, all very upper middle-class American family style. Well, I'd been dead wrong, because she didn't and that seemed to embarrass her some, too.

"Pardon the mess," she kept saying. "This place is a disaster, I know. I keep telling my mom we'd be a lot better off in a decent apartment somewhere than a crummy house like this."

The outside was pretty seedy. The inside, worse. The only room that was halfway decent was Susannah's. It was so frilly and fancy, and so neat and clean, it looked out of place in that house. It was pretty; that is, if you like rooms for Barbie dolls. Susannah hated it, though.

"It's my mother's idea of a room every sixteen-year-old girl in America ought to be dying to have, pink and white flowers, ribbons, ruffles, stuffed animals, yugg! She copied the whole thing from a decorating magazine, even the furniture, and it cost her a mint, so I have to pretend I'm crazy-wild about it. But it's so awful, so totally un-me. Not like your room, which is definitely yours, as anyone who knows you even a little can tell at a glance."

"My mother and I don't have much of a relationship," she confessed unhappily. "We don't communicate. Not like you and your mom."

"What makes you think my mom and I have such a great relationship?" I asked.

"Well, even if it's not, at least you communicate. You *talk* to one another, and that's what matters. My mother and I can't seem to do that. She doesn't want to hear what I have to say or know how I feel about things. She wants to believe what *she* wants to believe. She's got this image of me, and it's not the real one, but it's the one she prefers to live with, I guess. My mom's had a tough life. I guess it's left its mark. She's tired, bitter, all used up, and she doesn't want to put out any more effort than she has to."

I nodded, knowing what she meant. "So, when you have a problem and need someone to go with it, who do you go to?" I asked.

"No one. Myself, I guess. And now, you."

I smiled, feeling gratified. "I'm honored," I said. Susannah went to the sewing table and gathered up the fabric for my dress. "You've cut it out already?" I said, watching her lay the pieces of my dress out on the bed.

"Sure. That's a snap. Took me all of twenty minutes."

"Now I *am* impressed! What happens next?"

"We pin it together, baste it, then fit it on you."

In a few minutes, all the pieces of the dress were pinned and basted, and I was wearing them. Susannah made it all look so easy. I knew it wasn't, or at least wouldn't have been for me. Her hands were so nimble, so agile, and adept. I watched her pinning and tucking, creating a dress out of what had been just pieces of fabric, and thought to myself, *That's real talent, even if she doesn't know it.*

At about five-thirty, Mrs. Ellis arrived home. I was nervous about meeting her for the first time, and I think I made a fool of myself. Mrs. Eillis was the exact opposite of what I'd been expecting. I suppose I was expecting her to be beautiful like

Susannah, but she wasn't. If I was plain, she was plainer. Her gray hair was combed back in an austere style; her face completely devoid of any makeup. I caught myself thinking that wherever Susannah had gotten her looks, it certainly hadn't been from her mother.

I knew I ought to be getting home, but I couldn't leave right away and let Mrs. Ellis think it was on account of her. I stayed for a while, making strained small talk while Susannah went about starting dinner. I could feel Mrs. Ellis's reticence and the effort it took for her to converse, and it made me so tense, I wound up saying all the wrong things.

"I don't think she liked me," I whispered to Susannah when she was walking me to the door.

"She's thinking the same thing about you," Susannah whispered back. "You can't imagine how important that is to her, for you to like her. She wants us to be friends in the worst way. She thinks you're a good influence on me, and you *are*."

"How are the lenses working out?" my mother said when I got home.

"Okay," I replied, flopping down on the couch beside her. She was reading this book, something about the anatomy of the psychotic adolescent or something, and I could tell she was engrossed "I keep thinking I have something in my eye, though," I went on, wondering if she was even listening.

"You do," she mumbled, looking at me over the

92

book. "How's the dress coming along? Is it nice? I'm dying to see it."

"Mom, it's gorgeous!" I said, and went on to tell her all about the dress. "Susannah is really talented, you know it? She could have a future in fashion design someday."

"That reminds me," my mother said, reaching for the *Times*. "There's something in the newspaper today; something about some designing contest sponsored by the Fashion Institute. Now, where did I see that . . ." She started thumbing through the paper, mumbling to herself under her breath. Finally, she found what she was looking for and handed the paper to me.

"ATTENTION FUTURE FASHION DESIGNERS," the boxed ad read.

> *The Fashion Institute is sponsoring a contest to choose three talented high school students from the southern California area, all of whom will receive full scholarships to the Institute. For further information, write: Future Designers of America Contest, Box 444, Los Angeles, California, 90038.*

"Cut it out and give it to her," my mother said, going back to her book. "She might want to send for the information."

I was already tearing the ad out. "Never mind," I said, tucking it into my satchel for safekeeping. "Susannah has a habit of procrastinating about things. It'll be better if I just write away for her."

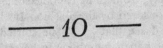

— 10 —

Next morning The Boy actually spoke to us, or rather to Susannah. Me, he ignored.

Standing in the middle of Magnolia, the two of them launched into this endless philosophical discussion about life, deciding the future of humankind, while I shifted impatiently from one blistered foot to the other, wishing they would fall in love already and get it over with so I could get home. The Boy's real name was Marc Lester. He was the actual son of *the* Matt Lester, the movie producer, and *the* Darcy Lester, movie director extraordinaire. Marc was a freshperson, literally and academically, at UCLA, where he was studying how to follow in his father's footsteps and become a rich and famous movie producer, too. He was telling Susannah about how he wanted to produce truly *meaningful* films for the good of all humankind.

Is this guy for real? I kept thinking.

From saving humanity, the subject then switched to the joys of jogging, wheat germ, unprocessed bran, and granola. I really couldn't believe Susannah was standing there looking lovesick over a creep like this. Finally, when I couldn't stand another minute, I gave her a subtle hint, like, "Suze, will you please move? We're going to be late for school!"

"Why don't we meet tomorrow," the boy prodigy suggested, "and, since it's Saturday, and none of us has school, why don't we have breakfast together at Solly's?"

"Okay!" I said, feeling about 0.3 percent better about him. I really like Solly's. My parents and I go there a lot. We took off for home with Susannah bringing up the rear for once instead of me.

"Isn't he *gorgeous*?" she sighed.

"You're both gorgeous. You're gorgeous together, a gorgeous couple, like you see in the magazines, The Beautiful People of sunny southern California. Even if you didn't dig each other, you'd have to go out. You owe it to the American public."

When we got to school, Susannah took off for her homeroom, in the throes of her romantic ardor, and I headed for mine. "Good luck on the English exam!" I called back to her.

She let out a large groan and said, "I forgot about that!"

I was a little late getting to English because of a run-in with a stuck locker. When I got there, Ms. Hartley was already passing out the test papers.

"Nice of you to join us, Allison," she said, slapping one in my hand as I charged past her desk.

"Sorry I'm late. Stuck locker," I mumbled, looking around for Susannah.

"Likely excuse!" Ms. Hartley said, grinning at me.

"A piece of cake," I whispered to Susannah as I passed her desk.

Ms. Hartley heard and called after me, "For you, a piece of cake. For everyone else, melba toast!"

"How did you do?" I asked, racing over to Susannah the minute the period was over.

"I don't know," she replied. "It was pretty hard."

Ms. Hartley was looking over the papers. "I'll correct yours now, so you won't have to be on pins and needles any longer," she said to Susannah. Two minutes later she waved Susannah's test paper in the air. "Seventy-eight. Hooray! Not too shabby for the girl whose last exam mark was a fifty. This reciprocal trade thing you girls have got going might just work."

"I don't believe I did that," Susannah said to me when we were walking to our next class. "Seventy-eight! I know, to you that's practically failing, but to me it's like getting a hundred."

"Don't knock it. Seventy-eight's beautiful," I said, feeling sensational in the extreme. "Well, we did it. And you just took your first step toward being another student type, like me, your egghead friend. Oh, gosh, I almost forgot to tell you. This is one very auspicious day in your young

96

life, you know it? All sorts of unreal things will happen to you because of this particular day."

"Yeah? Like what?"

"Well, like your grades are going to zoom sky high, for one thing. And, for another, you may just be on your way to becoming a future fashion designer of America. See, there's this contest, sponsored by the Fashion Institute. It's called the Future Fashion Designers of America Contest. I entered you."

"You *what*?"

"Well, no, I didn't really enter you actually. What I did was send for the information and an application so you could enter yourself."

I explained all about the contest and the scholarships, thinking she would be thrilled to pieces and terribly grateful, but it turned out she wasn't at all. In fact, she seemed annoyed.

"Next time, ask me before you do a thing like that, okay?" she said, turning and walking away, heading for her next class. I headed for mine, feeling a little put out. I mean, she ought to have been grateful to me for caring enough to do that for her, but she was acting as though I'd done something wrong. Later, when I met her for lunch, she slipped an arm through mine, acting real repentant, and said, "I didn't mean to be nasty before. I was feeling scared, that's all. It was really super, your thinking about me, taking the time to send away for that stuff. Don't think I don't appreciate it."

"I only did it because I have so much faith in you," I said, feeling a whole lot better. "And you weren't nasty to me before. Not really. Just a little short, that's all. I understood."

"I hear you and Bobby are going out Saturday night," Trisha said, smirking her way past us into the cafeteria. I couldn't believe it. Here Bobby and I hadn't even gone out on our first bonafide date yet, and already Leland's leading gossip monger knew all about it.

"Did you tell Trisha we were going out Saturday night?" I said to Bobby when he came along a couple of minutes later.

"Uh-uh. No way," he said, taking my books from me and dumping them on our favorite table.

"How did she find out then?"

"Beats me! Hey, maybe Lori told her. Lori asked me to come to a party Saturday night. I said no, I couldn't, and she asked why not, and I said because I had a date to go to the movies with you. Do you think Lori might've told Trisha?"

"Well, naturally, dopey. They're only inseparable. Lori is Trisha's leading source of information around here. Well, we might as well face it. By the end of lunch, the whole school will know we're going to a movie."

"So? What's the big deal? I don't care who knows. Do you?"

"No, not really."

"Well, no problem then." He handed me a tray, and we got on the lunch line. All the way down to the cashier, he was telling me about this gourmet meal he'd cooked the night before. "I'm turning into a master chef," he said, reaching for a container of milk. "The only thing is, after I get through making a meal, the kitchen looks like a disaster area. I can't figure out how my mom does it. When she cooks, there's not a crumb anywhere."

"Practice makes perfect," I said, helping myself to a fruit salad with cottage cheese and yogurt dressing, "and she's had plenty of practice. Say about twenty years' worth? Anyway, males are such total slobs. Females are much more capable and efficient."

He didn't say a word. We paid for our lunches and headed for the table. When we got there, he put his tray down, took mine from my hands and put it down, too, then pushed me down into the nearest chair and sat on my lap, threatening not to remove himself until I took what I said back and apologized.

"Okay, okay, I take it back. Help! You're squooshing me."

"No bodily contact in the cafeteria. That's the school rule." Susannah said, taking off for the lunch line.

After school, Susannah and I decided to go to Balboa Park to watch the roller skaters. She kept threatening to rent a pair of skates, but when we got there she chickened out. We were sitting on the grass, sharing a diet soda, when this baby blue pickup truck pulled into the parking lot.

"Aren't those the guys we met at the Promenade that day?" she said to me.

"I think so. I recognize Buffalo Bill."

"Fancy meeting you here!" the one named Scott said, ambling over to us. "It must be fate."

"Indubitably!" I said, looking at Susannah. She was looking at the one called Mitch and he was looking at her, and the way they were looking at each other, you expected sparks to start flying around any second. Scott sat down on the grass next to me and started coming on like gangbusters, doing this whole Mr. Smoothie routine that turned me off totally. I tried to make it obvious I wasn't interested, but he didn't take the hint. Susannah and Mitch seemed to be getting along famously, or anyway he was talking his head off to her, and she was listening to him, looking positively rapt. *Watch out, Mr. Beverly Hills!* I remember thinking. *You may just have competition.*

"Mitch is so nice," Susannah said when we were heading home.

"Scott isn't. He's a Marshall Medford in disguise. What was Mitch saying to you anyway? You looked so fascinated."

"Oh, just things like he wants to be a veterinarian, but his parents are pretty hard up for cash so he's not sure he'll make it. Did you give Scott your number?"

"No, did you give Mitch yours?"

"Yes, and he gave me his."

"And you're going to call him, of course."

"Of course not! You think I'm crazy? That's the last thing I need, a dirt poor cowboy!"

—— 11 ——

When we met Marc at Solly's the next day it was pretty crowded. Solly's is a super restaurant, kind of a combination deli and French bistro, where you can get anything from bagels to vichyssoise (otherwise known as cold potato soup), health food, southern fried chicken, or pot roast.

Solly saw us, and we got a table right away. "Look who's here," he said, sitting down with us, "Miss Jogger — pardon me, I should say Ms. Jogger — and friends. You are getting better-looking every day, you know it? And your friend here isn't all that bad either!"

"A friend of yours?" Marc asked when Solly went away.

"My folks and I eat here a lot. My mom sort of saved his son's life, and Solly worships her."

Susannah said to me, "So, since you're a steady customer, what do you suggest we order?"

"The Solly Special, definitely. It is the end!"

101

"Share one with me?"

"No way! I want a whole one for myself."

"I'll share," Marc said, checking out the menu. When the waitress came, he gave her our order, sounding as though giving orders was something he did a lot. While we were waiting for our food, he told Susannah and me about this film he was working on, something about the life and times of a twenty-year-old conscientious objector disguised as a rich kid living in Beverly Hills. I suddenly realized, when he was describing this scene he was shooting, that the equipment he was using wasn't at some studio somewhere or at his school, but at his house, or rather, mansion. From the way Marc described this enormous extravaganza his family lived in up in the canyon, it definitely was a mansion, not just a house. It really knocked me out, realizing that the location he was using for his scene was his own backyard, complete with swimming pool, stables, and tennis courts, and that the screening room he described wasn't at Universal or MGM, but in his own house.

He asked Susannah to go out with him that night, and she said yes. I wondered where he was planning to take her, to some swanky disco on Sunset Strip, probably, or maybe out to some expensive restaurant for a romantic candlelit dinner. You wouldn't expect someone like Marc Lester to just take a girl to a movie, right? You could see he really was taken with her, I guess that's the word to use, because he lined up a date for the next night, too, something about a movie premiere he and his folks were going to in Hollywood.

102

"A premiere?" she said, trying to be blasé, but I could tell what she was thinking. A little nobody, a high school girl, attending a Hollywood premiere, *and* with a famous producer and director. Our food came, and Solly came over to make sure everything was all right. We all went into ecstasies over the omelettes, and he went away happy. Susannah started telling Marc about the design contest. I think she was trying to let him know she wasn't exactly a total nobody, that she had something going for her, too.

"Are you really good?" he asked her.

"I think so," she replied, trying to be modest.

"You *think* so? Come on, Susannah!" I said, adding for Marc's benefit, "She's just stupendous, that's all."

"My mother's friend's a designer," Marc said to Susannah. "She's the owner of this company, Holly Go Lightly. Have you heard of it?"

"Holly Go Lightly?" Susannah exclaimed, really overwhelmed. "Marc, that's one of the best sportswear lines in L.A. I love their stuff!"

"And if Susannah says she loves it, you know it's got to be good," I said.

I saw him reach for her hand under the table. "Maybe I could get you together with my mother's friend sometime," he said, moving a little closer.

I was excited about the prospect, but I just wished I wasn't getting all these negative vibrations from Marc Lester. I wished I could like him, at least a little. There was just something so — I don't know — sort of phony and sneaky about him, at least that's the impression I got. Watching him feed her a bite of the omelette, I thought to myself, *Maybe it's just my overactive imagination at work, but I don't trust this guy.*

When we got to my house, the stuff from the Fashion Institute had come in the mail. "It says you're supposed to submit two outfits you made yourself, plus four sketches of original things you designed," I said, checking out the application form.

"That's no problem. I've got two dozen outfits, and sketchbooks full of original stuff."

"So, why don't we go to your house and get going on it," I suggested, watching her face. "Like my father always says, the early bird catches the worm."

"Who wants a worm?" she said, giving me a disgusted look. I figured that was it, that I could forget about the contest, but a few minutes later, when we were up in my room, she said, "You're right. Let's go. I'd better do it now before I change my mind." And we took off for her house.

There were so many stupendous things in her wardrobe, it really was a problem, deciding which to submit. We finally decided on this terrific suit.

"That one outfit is a whole wardrobe," Susannah said to me. "See, if you were going away for a weekend, that would be all you'd have to take, and an extra shirt, and maybe a sweater, and you'd be all set."

The second outfit was a tuxedo, a 1940s-looking number with big, wide shoulders, wide lapels of black satin, baggy trousers with a high waistband and lots of pleats, and a black satin stripe down the sides. With it Susannah had made a ruffled and pintucked man's evening shirt, a cerise satin bow tie and matching cummerbund, and this little evening vest, a black satin background with all this oriental embroidery on it.

We were getting everything packed up to send when the phone rang. Susannah picked it up, glanced over at me, looking kind of guilty, I remember thinking, and said in this guarded tone, "Yeah, well I just got home. Sure I did! Of course. I always do. No, I can't. And you can't either. No. Please don't push it, because I definitely can't, and I can't explain why either. No."

She hung up, and I said to her, "Who was that?"

"Oh, nobody you know," she said with a shrug. "Just some guy, that's all. He keeps calling me. He won't give up. I keep telling him I'm not going to see him. Some guys just never take no for an answer." A horn honked outside, and she said, "That's my mom with the groceries. I'd better help her."

"Do you think Susannah's doing the right thing, entering this contest?" Mrs. Ellis asked me when we were in the kitchen, and I was helping put the groceries away, what there was of them. With both of them on diets, it was mostly low fat cottage cheese, low calorie canned fruit, and diet soda. Not the best-balanced diet around. My mom would have had a fit if I ever brought that artificially sweetened stuff in the house.

"I think she is," I said, checking out the list of ingredients on a canned-fruit label. "She's awfully talented, Mrs. Ellis. This could be a great break for her."

"You really think she could win?" she said, giving Susannah a sidelong look that spoke volumes.

"Why not? She's good enough. How many kids could there be as good as she is?"

"At least five hundred in Tarzana alone," muttered Susannah, ramming a carton of eggs into the refrigerator with such a vengeance, I was expecting them to splatter all over the place.

"Well, all I can say is, I'm just glad you've got Allison for a friend," Mrs. Ellis said to her. "You never would have entered this contest if not for her."

When Mrs. Ellis had gone to her room Susannah said, "She thinks it's too late for her." Susannah sighed. "I suppose that's why she keeps constantly reminding me why it's so crucial to think ahead, about my future, because I'm her only chance. She can see the mistakes *she* made corrected if I avoid making them."

"It's a burden," I said, "having a parent so fixated on you. It would help if you had a sister like I do. That's the one thing I'll always be grateful for, that my sister Andrea was always there before me, kind of paving the way, making it easier for me. Of course, she's a hard act to follow. That's always been a problem, but my parents, being the way they are, would really have driven me berserk if I'd been an only child. I really want you to meet Andrea when she comes home next time," I added with a grin. "I'm dying to see what you think of her. Actually, aside from the fact she thinks she's Miss America, she's pretty okay."

"If she's anything like you, I'll love her!" Susannah exclaimed, smiling at me.

"Like me? Very funny! Andrea and I are complete opposites. She's pretty, gregarious, popular, and I . . ."

"Uh-uh-uh!" Susannah warned, shaking a finger under my nose. "Don't you dare put yourself down, on pain of death. That's your whole problem, I bet, this inferiority complex you have about yourself. You probably grew up thinking this sister of yours was Miss Perfect and you could never live up to her."

My parents are always very solicitous of my poor, undermined ego, taking pains never to do or say anything to damage the poor thing, but I always know what they're thinking. How can they help it when Andrea and I are so totally unalike? "We have the same parents. I can't figure out how we came out so totally different," I added with a rueful smile. "It's like she got all the good stuff, and I got shortchanged."

"If you ever say that in front of me again, I'll skin you," Susannah said, staring at me. "You are terrific. You are sensational, even if you don't know it, and I don't want to hear you put yourself down."

"You don't, huh? But you do it all the time, put yourself down, I mean," I said, grinning at her.

"You know," she said, changing the subject and glancing at the clock, "I'm still not sure what I'm going to wear tonight. I want Marc to be impressed, but I don't want to wind up sitting in a movie somewhere looking like Mata Hari."

"A movie? You don't think Mr. Beverly Hills is going to take you to a movie, dummy! He's probably planning on escorting you to some fantastic disco somewhere."

"Allison," she said, grinning at me. "I still can't believe it, me going out with Marc Lester. Who knows where it could lead? If he really likes me, we could wind up engaged or something. Then I wouldn't have to listen to my mother carrying on about my long-lost future anymore. I'd *have* a future if I married Marc."

I didn't say anything, but I was thinking to myself, *A future like that I could easily live without, even if he does have all that money and prestige and stuff.* "Listen, I don't mean to be nosy," I said, unable to stand the suspense any longer, "but who was the guy who called you before? Anyone I know?"

She shook her head. "No. Just some guy I met somewhere. Not anyone important. Not anyone who's a likely prospect, like Marc is. He's sort of cute, if you like the type, but let's face it, with all Marc has going for him, I'd have to be crazy to waste any time on anyone else."

— 12 —

Bobby picked me up around a quarter to seven.
We went to Hunan Garden, this Chinese restaurant in Chatsworth. He ordered a feast, enough
for six people easily — egg roll, dim sum, Moo
Shu Pork, shrimp in lobster sauce, fried rice. I
was starved when we sat down, but I was stuffed
to the gills halfway through the Moo Shu Pork,
so Bobby wound up finishing the rest of my
dinner along with his.

"I wish I could get into being a veggie," he
said, spearing the last grain of rice on his plate.
"Judy's a veggie. She hasn't eaten meat, fish, or
chicken for a year."

"Oh, wow! I don't think I could do that," I said.
Judy again! What was it with this Judy person
anyway? Was she somebody to worry about? I was
beginning to think so.

When we got to the movie theater, there was a

long line out front. We got on the end of it, and standing right ahead of us were The Terrible Two-some, Marshall and Trisha.

"Well, if it isn't the lovebirds," Marshall said to Bobby and me.

While we sat waiting for the first feature to begin, I was thinking about Susannah, wondering where she was at this exact moment and whether she was having a good time. I spotted Trisha and Marshall sitting in the center section across the aisle, spying on us. "If they could, they'd probably spend the evening watching *us* instead of the movie," I said to Bobby.

He glanced over at them, slipped an arm around me, and said, "Might as well give them something to watch, huh?" Then, just like that, he pulled me close and kissed me right there in the movie theater, with the lights still on, and not only Trisha and Marshall watching us, but the popcorn-sharing chubby couple next to us, and maybe a lot of other people, too, for all I knew.

"Well, that was nice!" I said when he let me go.

"I was hoping you'd think so."

"I didn't mean it that way."

"Oh, well, I can do better. Wait, I'll show you."

"Not now!" I whispered, glancing around. "Honestly, you're the least self-conscious human being I ever met."

"I'll take that as a compliment. Who wants to be the most self-conscious, even a little bit self-conscious? Not me!"

The first feature came on, an old horror movie about some guy who lives in a sewer, and haunts an opera theater wearing a cape and a mask. It was supposed to be terrifying, but I thought it was funny, more a comedy than a horror story.

On the way out of the theater, we ran into The Terrible Twosome again. "Want to go to Farrell's for a pig-out, or out for pizza or something?" Marshall asked. Bobby and I both said no, really emphatically, too, at the same time. Bobby said he was hungry again and suggested we go to Farrell's anyway, but I said no, we ought to go to my house and have some of the chocolate layer cake Helga had baked surreptitiously, while my mom wasn't looking. Bobby wound up devouring half the cake, plus a quart of milk. We went into the den, ostensibly to watch TV. I started getting kind of tense, waiting for him to make his move.

"You're waiting for me to make my move, aren't you?" he said, grinning away, looking pleased with himself.

"No, I'm not. What makes you say that?"

"Oh, come on, you're dying for me to kiss you, right?"

"Oh, brother! Talk about unemancipated. Listen, if kissing was what I had in mind, I wouldn't bother to wait for you to make your moves. I'd just grab you and kiss you if I felt like it."

"Really? So why don't you?"

I gave him a look. "Are you daring me or what?"

"No, just being emancipated. Are you going to kiss me or not?"

"All right. I will," I said, and *did*, much to my own surprise, and I think, his.

"Not half bad," he said, looking thoughtful, as though he was assessing the kiss on a sliding scale of one to ten. "But try putting a little more feeling into it. You know, some more emotion," he said, kissing me back. "See? Wasn't that better?"

"What is this, a kissing lesson? I know how to kiss. I don't need instructions."

"Am I implying you do? You do fine, only I'm just showing you a slightly different approach, that's all. A different technique, as it were. Look, did you like that, or should I try something else?"

"Oh, honestly! You really are outrageous," I said, and broke up laughing. It started out as kidding around, but before I knew it, by the next commercial break in the movie on TV we were ostensibly watching, the kissing was getting pretty serious, and we weren't just kidding around anymore. Frankly, if my parents hadn't chosen that exact moment to make their appearance at the love scene of the century, who knows what might have transpired? Anyway, it would have been a whole lot better than the one on TV.

"What are you watching?" my father said, coming into the den, my mom hard on his heels, both of them looking expectant, plus a little uptight, as though they were positive they'd be walking into a passionate necking session or something.

"An old movie," I replied, and started telling him all about it.

"How'd you manage *that*?" Bobby asked when they went upstairs.

"Easy, since I saw it three times before."

"Oh! I thought maybe you were watching it while I was kissing you, which would've been a pretty good trick, considering your back was to the set." He checked his watch. "Wow! Almost two o'clock. I'd better split. Who knows whether The Diapered Avenger might wake up in the small hours and shriek his head off to have his diaper changed."

I kissed him good night, then headed upstairs, feeling euphoric. "Allison Loves Bobby!" I wrote on my blotter, then next to that, "Bobby Loves Allison!" I was dying to phone Susannah, but I knew her mom would have conniptions, so I went to bed instead. I was just snuggling down under the covers, getting comfortable, thinking about Bobby, when the phone rang. I grabbed it fast so it wouldn't ring again.

"How about us going to the beach tomorrow?" Bobby whispered.

"The beach? Okay, sure," I whispered back.

"Pick you up around ten, okay? Hey, by the way, I meant to tell you before. In addition to your many other talents, you sure are a talented kisser, Al!"

"So? Tell all," Susannah said when I phoned her first thing next morning. "Did you have a super time?"

"Super? That's not even the word," I replied,

and went on to tell her every detail of the evening. "Now it's your turn," I said when I had brought her up to date. "How about Marc? Did you have a good time? Where did he take you, to some disco in Beverly Hills?"

"No, to the movies in Westwood. We kept running into people he knew from school. I was so uptight!"

"Why? What've you got to be uptight about? They're just people."

"Smart people. Educated people. People who're in college, which means they're in a whole other league from me."

"Susannah, that's ridiculous, and you know it! They're still just people. What d'you think they spend their time doing, sitting around in libraries, discussing Eastern philosophies and Western religion? Just because they're in college, that doesn't mean they're not into the same things we are, dating, clothes, food. So, are you still in love or what?"

"I'd be crazy not to be, wouldn't I?"

"Who's asking the questions around here? You or me?"

"Well, of course I'm still in love. How could I help it? He's not though. I'm sure. I mean, he could get any girl he wants. Why should he be in love with me?"

"Because you're gorgeous and sensational! How's that for starters?"

"He did ask me to go out again next weekend. That's a good sign, isn't it?"

"Well, it's certainly not a bad one! Susannah, what would it take to convince you? A marriage proposal?"

"Well," she said, laughing, "it would be a good start."

—— 13 ——

"**Y**ou're not wearing your lenses to the beach, are you?" my mom said when I came downstairs.

"No way! Gosh, why would I do that?"

"Well, I just wanted to make sure. Those lenses cost a fortune. What time is Bobby picking you up?"

"Any minute, I guess."

"Well, have a good time." She started to walk away, then turned back, looking at me with this odd, searching expression. "You really like him, don't you?" she said.

I was a little embarrassed. "Yes, I really like him, but don't worry. This is not some lowlife who's going to take advantage of your pure, innocent baby daughter. It's good, dependable, reliable, upstanding Bobby."

"Now, what was that all about?" she said, star- at me. "Who said anything about my being worried?"

"I just remember how you always were about Andrea, that's all."

"About Andrea? Allison, Andrea was impossible! She was unreliable, thoughtless, inconsiderate, and not only that, she lied. All the time in fact. She would tell us she'd be home by twelve, then show up at four A.M., at which time we were out of our minds with worrying. I certainly wouldn't expect to have to go through the same terrible phase with you. You're about the most dependable, considerate person I know. I trust you, Allison, because you've shown me I can. That's the difference between you and Andrea. I trust you, and I couldn't trust her!"

"You mean, you recognize she has a few faults?" I said, totally overwhelmed at this sudden revelation on my mom's part. "You mean, Andrea's not perfect after all?"

"Perfect? Do you think there's anybody who's perfect, Allison?"

"Well, I always thought you thought Andrea was."

"Do you know that's precisely what Andrea's always saying? That she always thought we thought you were. When it comes to bringing up children, one thing I've learned. You can't win either way. One is always sure you prefer the other, and vice versa."

"Well, what do you know?" I mumbled, shaking my head in perplexity. "I swear, Mom, I was always sure you thought Andrea was an angel from heaven, and I was the bad kid on the block. Why didn't you let me in on this a little earlier? I mean, at least then I would have had half a chance of growing up without an Andrea complex!"

She laughed, shaking her head at me. "You know, that's one of the things I love about you, your sense of humor. Unique, original, but definitely a trifle twisted."

I went into the kitchen to get myself something to eat. It was all too much to assimilate all at once. Next thing I knew, my mother would be telling me Andrea wasn't dying to be a doctor, or that she hadn't been elected Most Popular Girl in her class three years in a row. Or that she wasn't even my real, biological sister, but someone they adopted.

It was a perfect beach day, clear and pretty hot for that time of year. The water was cold as anything, sixty-five degrees, but the waves were just right for bodysurfing, so we went in anyway. We stayed in for ages, then lay out on the beach and worked on our tans. We walked up the Pacific Coast Highway to the frogurt stand for lunch and had homemade peach frogurt with granola, coconut, and strawberry syrup on top, then hiked back to the beach and swam again. The sun started to go down, and suddenly we were freezing.

"Why don't we change?" Bobby said. "We'll have pneumonia if we drive home in these wet suits."

He went to the men's bathhouse and I went to the women's, and we yelled back and forth to each other through the thin partition.

"Great day!" he said.

"Yeah, sensational!"

"This could get to be a habit, you know it, Al?"

"What, going to the beach?"

"No, dummy, you and me."

"Oh!"

"So? What d'you think?"

"What do I think about what?"

"About what I just said, us getting to be a habit."

"Oh! I don't know what I think. I haven't thought about it."

"Think about it now, okay?"

"Okay."

A couple of seconds elapsed, during which I stood there, dumbfounded. "So? Have you thought about it or what?" he called to me.

"Bobby," I squeaked, "what do you want me to say?"

"How about yes?"

"Yes, *what*?"

" 'Yes, Bobby, I'll go steady with you,' that'd be good for starters."

After all these years, fantasizing about his asking me that question, now that he actually had, I was in shock, too numb to react or feel anything. What a weird place for a love scene, a public bathhouse on a beach at Malibu! How many couples decide to go steady through a bathhouse wall, for gosh sakes?

"Well?" he said, and I could hear the tension in his voice.

"Well," I murmured, leaning my forehead against the slatted wood partition. "Yes, I guess. Yes, Bobby, I'll go steady with you."

119

I heard a door slam. Hurriedly I pulled my jeans up over my hips, zipped them, pulled my sweatshirt over my head, grabbed my towel and my beach bag, and flung myself out the door. Bobby was standing there, looking kind of overwhelmed and blushing.

"Congratulations," he said, taking a step toward me. "I hear you're officially going steady." Then, with a triumphant yell, he grabbed me, pulled me into his arms, and kissed me.

—— *14* ——

"You know what? You're pretty weird!" I said when I got into the car.

"You're just finding that out after all this time?"

I nodded, smiling. "Mind if I venture one question? How come you never asked me out before now?"

He turned the key in the ignition. The battered, old Chevy coughed into action. "Don't think I didn't want to," he said, turning to look over his shoulder as he backed the car out of the parking space. "It's just that I never figured you'd want to go out with your old chum, Bobby, the kid you've known ever since kindergarten. I mean, I'm not so overflowing with ego that I was in shape to get turned down, so I guess I just let it ride, figuring sooner or later I'd get around to it. If Susannah hadn't let me know you'd be receptive, I guess I'd still be deliberating: Should I or shouldn't I? Will she or won't she?"

"Susannah did *what*?" I asked, staring at him.

He swung the car around, stepped on the brake, and turned to me with a comic expression. "Oh, wow! I promised not to say anything about that. Listen, just don't tell her, okay? She'll kill me."

"I don't believe this," I muttered as he pulled out of the parking lot. "I just don't *believe* this! Who does she think she is, my fairy godmother?"

"Something like that, I guess. Hey, if she hadn't said anything, we wouldn't be here now. So we ought to be grateful, right? That's what we needed, you and I, someone to play fairy godmother, or rather, Cupid."

"You're right, I suppose, but what if you didn't want to ask me out? It would've been darned embarrassing, for me, anyway. You know, she really does care about me, or she wouldn't have gone out on a limb for me like that. I'm very grateful we got to be friends. She's done a whole lot of things for me nobody else ever would have; things I certainly wouldn't have known enough to do for myself either."

He nodded, keeping his eyes on the road as he maneuvered the hairpin turns on the Malibu Canyon Road. "It's not exactly a one-sided relationship either, Allison. You've done something terrific for her, too. She told me about the English exam. All in all, it's pretty much of a reciprocal thing!"

"I suppose," I mused, snuggling beside him, "but I just have the feeling it's me who's getting the better end of the deal."

The instant I got home, I phoned Susannah.

"You sneak! How *could* you? What if he hadn't wanted to ask me out? Did you even think of that?"

"Of course I did," she replied in an offhand tone, acting as though playing Cupid was her true role in life. "That's just why I asked him first."

"Asked him?"

"Listen, what's wrong with that? All I said was, 'Am I imagining this, or is there something going on with you and Allison?' He said, 'Well, I don't know how Allison feels, but with me there is.' Then I asked him why he hadn't asked you to go out with him. When he said he hadn't because he wan't sure you would want to, I suggested he give it a try because I had the feeling you would. Look, what are you getting uptight about? It worked out, didn't it? I mean, if somebody didn't do something, you two guys would never have gotten around to it."

"Susannah, I don't believe you. This could've been a disaster."

"Well, it wasn't. I mean, isn't. Listen, want to go out for something to eat? My mom's not home, and I don't feel like sitting here all by myself eating bird food. Why don't I come over, and we'll go get some pizza or something?"

She drove over and collected me, and we went to Encino to The Little Old Pizza Maker and had an Everything On It, complete with pepperoni, mushrooms, sausage, anchovies, the works. I felt guilty about indulging in all those calories, but Susannah said we'd jog it off next morning, so with that in mind I got carried away with myself and really gorged.

"You know," she said, nibbling on the crust of the last piece, "I'm so nervous about tonight, I'm freaking out completely. All those celebrities, the gorgeous clothes and all. I'm going to look like a hick. I wish I hadn't said I'd go. I must have been crazy!"

"Susannah, that's dumb," I said, patting my overstuffed belly. "You just don't *see* yourself, that's your problem. You can hold your own with any gorgeous celebrity movie star, and I'm not just saying that because I'm your friend. For one thing, you're more beautiful than nine-tenths of those movie stars, and for another, it's not as though you don't know the first thing about fashion. You probably know tons more about fashion than all of them put together."

"Allison, Marc's so, well, smart and sophisticated, and I'm so . . . so *nothing*! I don't know anything. I'm not well-informed on any subject except fashion and stuff. I never know what to say to him. And to make it worse, his parents will be there. If I'm uptight making conversation with him, imagine how I'm going to feel with his parents! What can I talk about? Aside from the length of hemlines this season and what manufacturer is coming out with which new style, that's all I know."

"Look, let me give you some advice. You know how to listen? Good! 'Cause that's all you really have to do to make a hit with his parents."

"Just listen? Allison, are you sure?"

"Yes, I am. That's the key word, *listen.* These

people are so egocentric, all they want to do is talk about themselves. So if you just sit there, look pretty fascinated by every word they utter, and smile a lot, they'll love you. They'll go around saying how brilliant you are, and you won't have said a single word the whole time."

"You really think that?"

"Definitely! Look, another thing. Do you think a guy like Marc Lester is going to go out of his way to take a nothing to a Hollywood premiere? The guy *does* have an ego, and he likes people to see him in a certain way. Right? So why would he take a girl who would stick out like a sore thumb, especially with his illustrious parents along for the ride? By the way, I meant to ask. What are you wearing?"

"My gray chiffon. It's pretty clingy, but it's the look I want, kind of halfway between sexy and demure. I want Marc's parents to take one look at me and say, 'That's the girl we want for our daughter-in-law!' "

"What?" I stared at her, aghast. "Their daughter-in-law? Susannah, that's supposed to be a joke, isn't it? You're not serious!"

"Sure I'm serious. Why not? Look, Marc's the best thing that's ever happened to me, and don't think I don't know it. I'm not about to blow it if I can help it. I have no real future, Allison, My mother's right about that. I'm obviously not going to go to college, and what skills do I háve? I can either take typing and shorthand, like my mother did, and wind up drudging away in an office somewhere as someone's secretary or slave, or become a gifted waitress or a clerk in a store somewhere, selling lingerie or shoes. Not exactly every girl's dream, huh? But Marc *is*."

"Every mother's, too," I muttered, thinking about Mrs. Ellis and what she would have to say to Susannah on the subject of Marc.

"Sure. My mother's on an all-time high about this, and why not? Whoever thought anything like this would happen to me? Talk about a future! He's in his third year at UCLA. We could get engaged right now if we wanted to. After all, his folks are loaded. He'll never have to struggle to support a wife. When he graduates next year, we could get married and live happily ever after. Think of what a life I'd have. And my mom. I could help her, too. She wouldn't have to knock her brains out in that dumb office anymore. She could have a little bit of fun before it's too late." Susannah looked a little chagrined. "She's only worried I'll do something to blow it. All she keeps saying to me is, 'Just be careful. Act like a lady. Don't say too much.' All sorts of motherly advice like that. I guess she's afraid if I open my mouth, Marc and his parents will find out how dumb I am."

"Terrific!" I muttered, making a face. "That must give you lots of confidence; make you feel real up and sure of yourself, your mother saying things like that to you."

On the way back to my house, I sat there thinking about Mrs. Ellis and how much more understandable Susannah's feelings about herself were now that I had met her. To Mrs. Ellis, Susannah's marrying at an early age would be a blessing, but to me it was a tragedy. Just the thought of what Susannah's future would be like made me shiver with dread. I turned to her and said, "You'll be angry at me for saying this, but the whole idea of your marrying Marc, now or later, is sick. You could have a great future, Susannah, or anyway, you can try instead of copping out at the first opportunity, settling for somebody else's future instead of going out there and fighting and working for one of your own."

Without another word, I got out of the car and marched off into the house, feeling a lot like Joan of Arc.

"Your lover boy called three times while you were out," Helga said when I walked into the kitchen. "He says you should call him right back."

"Helga," I said, giving her a hug, "you are adorable, and I love you with a passion!"

She disengaged herself, scowling at me, but I could tell she was pleased. "Excuse me, Miss. I don't like being pawed."

I went upstairs and phoned Bobby, and he asked if I felt like taking a ride. I was exhausted, but I said yes. I threw on a jacket, put on a drop of mascara and a little lipstick, "combed" my hair, and was ready and waiting six minutes later when he pulled up in front of the house.

"When you said let's go steady, I didn't think you meant twenty-four hours a day," I said as I climbed into the car.

He leaned over and kissed me, a quickie kiss on the cheek, then a not-so-quick kiss on the lips.

"Mmm, you taste good! Smell good, too. You know, I kind of like you. For a girl, you're all right."

"For a girl!" I cried, swinging at him, but he was ready for me, and he ducked. "Boy, you sure know the right buttons to push to get me going," I muttered, snuggling up to him. "Actually, I kind of like you, too. For a guy, you're not half bad yourself. There's something I've been wanting to tell you. It's really preying on my mind. I feel like I've got to say it. The truth is, I've been wild about you for the longest time."

"What? You have? I thought you just liked me as a friend. Why didn't you communicate this information to me, so we could've gotten together sooner? Think of all the time we wasted being friends. Hey, you know, you sure are a funny kid sometimes. You come off so, well, together, so aloof, and kind of sarcastic sometimes, like you think everybody else is beneath you. But you're not like that at all. You've got all these feelings hidden away inside. Not that I'm complaining, you understand. If I'm not bursting with self-confidence, it'd be kind of intimidating to be in love with a girl who was."

"In love?" I said, staring at him.

"In love. What else?"

I shrugged. "I don't know. That's not a word I use all that casually."

"Neither do I."

"Being in love, that means making a big commitment."

"Exactly!"

"I mean, you don't go around saying 'I love you' to just everybody."

"As a matter of fact, I've never said it to anybody before. Have you?"

"Just my parents actually."

"Allison, I guess I've loved you since we were five years old. What're you acting so surprised about? If I don't love *you*, who do I love?"

"I don't know. Who do you?" I murmured, thinking of the mysterious Judy.

He glanced over at me. "Don't you . . . you know, feel the same way?"

I didn't answer right away. How could I tell him how I had felt all these years, loving him so desperately, but from afar, thinking there would never be anything more between us than just a platonic friendship? We parked at the lookout on Kanan Dume Road and sat there staring out over the canyon, just talking, but not looking at one another. It was funny. If you don't look at the person you're talking to, you can actually convince yourself there's no one there and you're talking to yourself. That made it easier. Some of the things I was saying were about as revealing as anything could be, and I wasn't all that used to baring my innermost soul to anyone.

"I'm so glad we talked," he murmured when we were pulling into my driveway. "I've never felt so close to anyone in my life. I really *do* love you, Al."

"I love you, too, Bobby," I murmured, putting my arms around him. Just then the floodlights in my next-door neighbor's driveway went on, il-

129

luminating the whole immediate world. The Porters had arrived home in their Jeep, all eight of them — two parents, six kids.

"I'd better split," Bobby said with a sigh, giving me a kiss that missed my mouth and wound up on the tip of my nose. "School tomorrow, and besides, better get some sack time while I can. The Monster has a new habit. It's called midnight tantrum."

"Oh, wonderful!" I laughed, kissing him back before I climbed out of the car. "I'm glad I don't live in *your* house. He pulled out of the driveway, and I went inside, bleary-eyed at this point after the long, active weekend. Come to think of it, I told myself as I dragged myself up the stairs, my weekends had never been anything to write home about until now, but this one had almost made up for all the others I'd missed over the years.

I sure hoped Susannah didn't get home too late. As much as I was dying to hear all about her evening, there was nothing I detested more than being wakened out of a good sleep, and tonight I knew I was going to sleep like a log, as my dad would have said.

Susannah called about one, just as I was dozing off. "It was unreal!" she said, sounding so up it made me feel up, too. "Just like on TV, a real Hollywood premiere, wall-to-wall celebrities."

She went on at great length, telling me about all the famous people she had seen, some of whom she had actually been introduced to in person. Finally, I said, "So, how are Marc's parents? Are they nice? Did you like them? Did they like you?"

130

"Well, I think so. At first I was nervous, but I kept thinking about what you said. You know, about keeping my big mouth shut and just listening, and it worked. Anyway, I think I really impressed them. I heard Mr. Lester tell Marc he thought I was charming and lovely, and Mrs. Lester, um, I mean Ms. Bremmer — she doesn't like you to call her Mrs. Lester — kept smiling at me the whole night, acting like she really thought I was terrific; like we were girlfriends or something."

"I'm proud of you!" I said. "So, when are you seeing him again, other than jogging, I mean?"

There was pause, after which Susannah hemmed and hawed for a time before blurting out, "Well, actually he invited me to spend next weekend at Arrowhead."

"Arrowhead? Oh, his folks have a house there?"

"No. *He* has."

"Oh-oh!"

"Yeah, I knew you'd say that. We both knew something like that would be forthcoming, didn't we? I mean, let's not be naive. Of course I'm not going, but I don't have to tell you that, do I?"

"Of course not!" I lied. "You don't have to tell me that."

— 15 —

Next day the four of us polished up our act for the Careers Day report. The whole time we were working, Marshall was acting so obnoxious. Finally, we all got disgusted and told him off. The committee meeting broke up with Marshall swearing he'd quit school before he'd work on that committee with us another second.

"Tomorrow he'll probably come skulking over to apologize, like he did that other time," Susannah said, staring after him.

"Maybe we ought to tell Ms. Dorcas what's going on," I suggested, relishing the idea.

"No, let's just leave it the way it is," Bobby said. "If he means it, and he really doesn't hang in, we'll go to Dorcas then."

Susannah and I were spending the afternoon studying Math, or anyway that's what was on the agenda. Only, it turned out, there were all these huge sales going on at the Promenade, so she talked me into dashing over there to check them out. I wound up getting a whole bunch of bargains, with the aid and support of my own personal bargain hunter. Looking at myself in the mirrors in the dressing room, I was thinking, *Hey, who are you, the girl with the waistline and the shoulder bones? Whatever happened to your pudgy cheeks, your chunky thighs, and that humungus rear end? Where'd you get that chic hairdo and those cheekbones? They never were there before. And as for those big, sexy, green cat's eyes, well, no wonder they're calling you the new sex symbol of Leland High!*

Susannah and I smiled at one another in the mirror. She was looking the way my dad always looks when one of his baby patients graduates from formula to whole milk with no ill effects.

"Not bad, huh?" she said.

"No, not at all bad," I replied, "thanks to you!"

We put in a couple of gruelling hours studying math, and I do mean gruelling hours! Let's face it, math was her worst subject. If I thought she was having trouble with some of her other subjects, math was hopeless. Nothing I did seemed to help her understand what it was all about. She just got more and more confused, and I got more and more discouraged. Finally, I decided to give up trying to make her understand, and took another tack.

"Okay, here's what we're going to do. You're not planning on making physics your future, right? Or being a mathematician or Nobel-prizewinning scientist? So you don't understand this stuff. Okay. You don't have to understand it. There's another way we can approach this, and it'll get you through the course with a passing grade. See, you'll just memorize a bunch of examples, one of every type in the course. When you take a test, you'll see an example on the test paper, and you'll think to yourself, 'Aha! This is just like Example A on that list my darling friend Allison made me memorize, so I'm going to tackle it the same way I do Example A, and that way I'll be sure to get it right!' See? You won't know what you're doing, but it won't matter, because you'll be doing it right anyway, and you'll pass!"

Math wasn't Susannah's forté, and committing things to memory wasn't either, as I soon found out. We worked and we worked, and I kept on testing her, and she kept on freaking out, getting so uptight and nervous, I figured by the time we were through she'd have a nervous breakdown and still not know the work.

"It gets easier as we go along," I said, trying to convince myself as well as her. "If we hang in, we can do it. You'll pass. Maybe not with flying colors, but you'll pass. That I promise!"

We went downstairs to have some iced tea, and she started to unwind a little. I felt so sorry for her. I'm not sure, if it was as hard for me as it was to her, that I would have hung in all that long. I mean, I like a challenge, but there is such a thing as too much of a challenge! I got the feeling she had something else on her mind besides math, because she kept dropping these not-so-subtle, little hints. I waited, figuring that sooner or later she'd come out with it, whatever it was, and of course ultimately she did.

"You know that guy I told you about who keeps calling me all the time?" she said, not looking at me. "It's someone you know. I lied when I said it wasn't."

"Why'd you do that?"

"I dunno. It's not someone from school, or anything like that. You have met him though. It's that cowboy, Mitch."

"Mitch? So why did it have to be such a deep, dark secret? It's not as though Jack the Ripper was making obscene phone calls to you."

"I just didn't want you to start hassling me to see him, that's all. And I knew you would."

"Who, me? Would I tell you who you ought to go out with?"

"Definitely!"

I grinned. "Well, he *is* nice. And cute! And you liked him. You told me so. So why do you keep turning him down, Susannah?"

"See? You're doing it," she mumbled, looking upset. "Look, I figure there's no sense my starting up, especially with someone like him; especially now that things are going so well with Marc and all. What would Mitch possibly have to offer me? Nothing! And Marc has everything to offer a girl. Just everything! I'd have to be crazy not to concentrate on him fulltime, like he's concentrating on me."

"How do you know Marc's concentrating only on you?"

"He told me. He told me he isn't seeing anyone else, and he asked me to do the same."

"Oh, terrific! Nothing like tying a girl up, is there? I bet I know why you didn't want to see

Mitch. You were afraid if you did, you'd fall for him, and that'd cause complications in your scheme to snare Mr. Beverly Hills! Susannah, money's terrific, sure. It's nice if you can have *it* and love, too, but I wouldn't build a relationship on just money."

"It isn't just money. It's the whole package deal," Susannah said, getting real defensive. "Marc's handsome. He's talented. He's going to be somebody someday. Anyway, I like him. I more than like him, in fact. If a girl had a guy like Marc, she'd really be somebody."

"Yeah, Mrs. Marc! That's what you want? To live off somebody else's glory? What if he walked out on you? What would you have then? You've got to make your own future, Susannah, have a life of your own." I looked at her, wondering if I'd said too much. She looked so unhappy, and it made me feel so bad. "So, when are you seeing Mitch?" I murmured, knowing darned well she was going to.

She looked up, smiled sheepishly, and whispered, "Tonight!"

Next morning it was jogging as usual. The minute she walked in my front door, I grabbed her and said, "Tell!"

"Oh, Allison, he's so sensational!" she breathed, and started rhapsodizing about Mitch. "He's so caring, so nice. He talks to me, really talks, and he listens. He doesn't just sit there staring at me, talking all about how beautiful I am and how he never went out with anyone so beautiful before.

He's interested in *me* as a person, not just a . . .
a . . ."

"An ornament?"

"Yes, right! An ornament, something to show
off to people. Oh, Allison," she moaned, acting as
though this was a tragedy, not a love story, "if it's
just as easy to fall in love with a rich guy as a
poor one, like my mother's always telling me,
why couldn't it be the other way around? Why
couldn't Mitch be the rich guy and Marc the cowboy who's dirt poor?"

"That'd be convenient. When are you seeing
Mitch again?"

"Tonight. And tomorrow night. Probably the
next night, too. He says he never felt like this
about any girl before; that he was starting to
think maybe he never would 'til I came along,
and it's the same with me, Allison. I was always
saying I was in love, but I never was. Not really.
Allison, if only we'd never met them that day at
the Promenade, life would be just so much less
complicated!"

"Life's supposed to be complicated, dummy!
Don't you know that?"

"Mitch is taking me to the beach next Sunday,"
she said. "We thought maybe you and Bobby
could come along, so the four of us could get together; you know, get to know one another. I want
you and Mitch to be friends. You're my best
friend, and Bobby's your boyfriend, and Mitch
is . . . is . . ."

"Yes?"

"Um, I don't know! Allison, what am I going to
do?"

"Just let it happen, then deal with it the best you can."

Susannah did her whole Super Jogger routine that day, putting on the speed, leaving me behind. Panting and gasping for breath, feeling as though I'd just run the Boston Marathon in two seconds flat, I chugged after her. When I caught up with her, there was Marc, jogging along with her. When we had done our usual route and were heading back down to Ventura Boulevard, Marc started talking about the upcoming weekend, making all these plans — what they were going to be doing together and all. Then he started planning all their weekends together, like for the next seventeen years, making it sound as though their relationship was permanent. Any minute I expected him to whip out a huge diamond ring and slip it on her dainty little finger and say "I do!" Frankly, how sensitive could he be if he didn't even notice how miserable and uncomfortable the girl was?

"I'm sorry, babe," he said, using one of my least favorite terms of endearment, "but I can't see you Friday night. I've got an exam Saturday morning, and I'm going to stay up all night studying."

He acted as though she ought to be desolate. When he had kissed her and jogged off, I said to her, "So, what're you going to do about Sunday? Ask him along?"

"If I had half an ounce of brains, I'd break the date with Mitch," she muttered, watching him jog away.

When we got to school, I headed for homeroom. Bobby came along behind me and kissed the back of my neck, and said, "I missed you," smiling at me in that special way, not the least self-conscious, though we were surrounded by people.

"I missed you, too," I said loud and clear. "Do you realize it's been twelve hours and twenty-four minutes since we last saw each other?"

"That's a long time. Want to go out for lunch today? I've got the car," he said, slipping an arm through mine as we walked down the corridor. "We could go to Señor Frog for tacos, and smooch."

"Wow, Mr. Moneybags! What's the occasion?" I laughed.

"*Us!*"

I felt my heart slipping around inside me. "Well," I said softly, almost too overwhelmed to speak at all, "that's certainly a cause for celebration if there ever was one. Okay, since we're celebrating us, I'll splurge and have one taco. I know I can count on you to eat the rest."

Señor Frog is just about the prettiest restaurant in the area, Mexican countrified with French overtones, quarry tile floors, whitewashed stucco walls, beamed ceilings, arches, antique furniture, and lush plants everywhere you look. Bobby ate five tacos. I ate two. We both drank about a gallon each of iced tea to quench the enormous thirsts worked up from all the hot tacos. Bobby made a toast with his iced tea glass, to us. We clinked glasses. I remember thinking that, the way he said, "To us," he made it sound as though he was planning on its being permanent. I was recalling all the impossible fantasies I used to indulge in about him that I never thought for an instant would ever come true: us getting married, going to live on some desert island somewhere, where he would run a whale-watching station and collect sea specimens, and we would spend all our days roaming the beaches, deep-sea diving, living this totally idyllic life together, two happy beach-combers without a care in the world.

— 16 —

"Why haven't I heard anything about that contest?" Susannah said when we were driving to school next morning. "It's been ages!"

"Ages? Susannah, it hasn't even been two weeks. It could take months before you find out. You can't drive yourself bananas like this worrying about it all that time."

"I know, but I can't stand the suspense. I wish I'd never let you talk me into entering that dumb thing in the first place. Who needs this? Haven't I got enough problems in my life already? Look, I know darned well I'm not going to win, but I can't help thinking a miracle could happen, and I might. And my mother's so uptight, she's practically having a nervous breakdown. It's not worth the hassles. It really isn't!"

"Would it be if you wound up winning?" I said, grinning at her. "You know darned well it would! Susannah, winning that contest is going to change the whole course of your life."

"Listen, did you ask Bobby about Sunday? The beach, I mean?"

"Oh, I forgot. Remind me later, okay? Like my dad's always saying, I'd forget my head if it wasn't screwed on tight."

We had a dress rehearsal for the concert that day; also a surprise math test. When Mr. Nordstrom announced it, I looked over at Susannah, who was looking at me with this horrified expression on her face that said, in essence, *"Help! Get me out of here."* Trying to be hugely reassuring, I smiled and made an A-okay sign in the air.

"Well, I see *somebody* isn't demolished by my announcement," Mr. Nordstrom said, giving me this amused look. "Is that an attempt at silent sarcasm, Ms. Lawrence, or do you just like taking exams?"

"That was hard," I said to Susannah when class was over, and we were walking out together. "I mean, *hard*! Did you remember any of the stuff we studied?"

She nodded. "At first I panicked, but then I started talking to myself, giving myself a pep talk, and you know what? It worked. Once I calmed down, it started to come back. That first question, was that like Example B in that list we worked on, or was I wrong?"

"It *was* Example B!" I exclaimed, stopping dead in my tracks. "Susannah, you did it. You got those things memorized without even realizing you did."

142

"No kidding? Really? I can't believe it. The minute I looked at it, I saw Example B in my head, so I did it the same way. I just hope I didn't goof on the calculations, that's all. I can't add or subtract to save myself, so I use my fingers and toes, and when I run out of them I'm in deep trouble. Gosh, I feel so happy, like I did something sensational, not just get one question right on a dumb, old math exam.

"You know," she went on, smiling at me, "this reciprocal trade agreement is working out. It may turn out to be the greatest thing that ever happened to me. Now we have to finish the dress for the concert," she said. "I'm going to call Mitch and tell him to cancel tonight. We've got to finish that dress."

"Couldn't we work on it after school?"

"Not enough time."

"Well, then tell Mitch to come to my house. He can keep us company, and we can work on the dress at the same time."

"Super! Why don't you tell Bobby to come over, too? We'll make it a double date."

"Susannah and her new boyfriend are coming over tonight," I said to Bobby when I saw him after fourth period. "Want to come over? If you're real nice to her, maybe Helga'll let you have some of that cake she baked last night."

"I'm sorry, Al. I promised Judy I'd go to this meeting with her. Some of the people from her chapter of the Sierra Club are getting together to try and stop the developers from moving into the Sepulveda Basin, and Judy thinks we all ought to get behind them and give them some support."

"Oh! Well, there's something else I was supposed to ask you. Susannah and Mitch are going to the beach Sunday. They wanted us to come along."

"Hey, gee, I feel terrible, but didn't I tell you? Sunday I'm supposed to go up to Pismo Beach to go clamming with Judy."

"Really? Well, have a super day!" I said in a wounded tone and stalked away, heading for my class. I don't know. Maybe I'm way out of line on this, but it's always been my belief that when a boy asks a girl to go steady, he means *steady*. In other words, it's not too much to expect that the girl he's going steady with won't have to share him with another girl. Anyway, that's what I've always thought. At that point, however, I was beginning to think it was an old-fashioned concept and no longer applied.

"Did you ask Bobby about Sunday?" Susannah said when I walked into social science.

I nodded. "Yes, but he's already got a date."

"What?"

"He's going to Pismo beach with someone named Judy. Judy, that's this girl he talks about all the time. Everytime you turn around, you have to hear about Judy. It's Judy this and Judy that. I get the feeling he ought to have asked *Judy* to go steady instead of *me*!"

"If he wanted to, he would have," she said, giving me a look. "A guy doesn't ask one girl to go steady if he digs another, dummy."

"No? Well, maybe you ought to tell Bobby that. Listen, ask Mitch about Scott, okay? Maybe he'd like to go to the beach with me Sunday."

"Allison, you're supposed to be going steady!"

I smiled "Really? Look, if Bobby can have a Judy, then *I* can have a Scott, or anyone else I feel like going out with, for that matter. This isn't the dark ages, you know, the pre-liberation days. It's a two-way street, as my father's always saying. I'm emancipated, aren't I?"

"Maybe too emancipated," Susánnah muttered, and headed for her desk.

Bobby came in, walked right up to me, and said, "What's bugging you? Would you mind telling me?"

I gave him a long look. "Yes."

"Allison, what'd I do? Why're you mad at me all of a sudden?"

"Well, if you must know, I think you've got some nerve asking me to go steady when you're not ready for that kind of commitment. You're entitled to play the field, if you want to. Only, I think you should have made that decision before you asked me to go steady with you."

I walked away, my nose in the air, and nearly collided with Siggy Mumbles and his tuba.

"Don't you think you ought to come out and just ask him who this Judy is?" Susannah said after school. "I mean, you're the one who's always carrying on about how crucial it is in any relationship to be up front and honest."

I tried to explain how I felt. How scared I was to ask, knowing deep down, what the explanation would be. I guess you could say I still felt that no matter what anybody said or how they acted, I really was unattractive and undesirable. That a boy, especially one like Bobby, couldn't possibly really want me. In my mind, Judy was the kind of girl Bobby really wanted, and I knew that in the end she was the one he would choose, leaving me out in the cold.

"I don't have to ask who Judy is," I sighed, shaking my head disconsolately. "Don't you think I know already? I've been hearing about her for weeks. Look, I can change the way I look to some degree, Susannah, but I can't change who I am deep down inside. Once Bobby spent some time finding that out, I knew he wouldn't stick around!"

She stared at me. "That's the craziest thing I ever heard! He already *knew* who you were deep down inside. You've been friends for years."

"Friends, that's the key word," I moaned, looking at her with pleading eyes. "No matter what you say on the subject, or how ultraliberated you are in your attitudes, a friend isn't a girlfriend. There's a big difference. As a friend I was okay, but as a girlfriend, obviously I fall short of the mark, or otherwise, would there be a Judy?"

"I can't take this," she grumbled, stalking away. "There's just no reaching you, Allison. You've got some kind of mental block. That's all there is to it. Your whole argument is totally unreasonable."

She turned back to stare at me, challenge in her eyes, and said, "You know the only reasonable, logical thing to do at this point is to go to Bobby and ask straight out, 'Who is this Judy person?' "

I dropped my eyes. "Why should I inflict more pain on myself by having him tell me all about her? I'm feeling lousy enough."

She stood there staring at me for a moment longer, pain in her eyes, then sighed and turned away, dejected. I started to call after her, but changed my mind. I could see the similarity between our situations all too clearly. I wondered whether she was right, if I did have a mental block that was making me misread the whole situation, keeping me from seeing it clearly; a mental block not unlike the one that was plunging her into a relationship that was wrong for her just because she didn't feel good enough about herself to believe she could make a future of her own.

I told myself to take her advice, go to Bobby and get it straightened out, but in the end I just couldn't do it. Thinking back, I truly believe it was just plain false pride that kept me from it; that and being stubborn. Anyway, now I wish I had, because in the end when the chips were down, it would have saved me a whole lot of needless pain and suffering.

If I had had any doubts about Susannah and Mitch, I was over them now, seeing the two of them together. This was it, the real thing. Anyone could see that. It was like one of those soppy love scenes in one of those corny, old movies. You know the kind, when the hero and heroine are suddenly alone in a room together, and they sit there gazing yearningly into one another's eyes, looking lovesick.

We never got to work on the dress. By the time Mitch left, it was too late. Susannah said she'd come over first thing next morning, and we'd finish it then. I told her not to clutch, that if we didn't get it done, I'd just wear the dress I had, the one I'd gotten for my cousin's wedding. I pretended it was no big thing, but to tell the truth, after all those weeks of following her around the stores, listening to her theories on haute couture, checking out all those gorgeous clothes and all, now I knew just what a fiasco that would be, and I wasn't too delighted at the idea of the image I would present in that corny dress.

"Never fear. Susannah's here," she said, reading my mind. "You will wear that dress to the concert and be so chic, every girl in town will be eating her heart out."

I was just crawling into bed that night when the phone rang. Figuring it must be Susannah, calling to reassure me once again about the dress, I picked it up and said, "Hi!" in this real friendly tone.

"Allison?" Bobby said a little hesitantly.

I froze. "What's on your mind? I was just going to bed."

His voice took on an edge. I could tell he was angry. "What do you mean, what's on my mind? What do you think? Look, something is bugging you. You're mad as hell at me, and I think I'm entitled to know why. I thought we had a relationship going here. Now I'm beginning to wonder."

"Well, I thought we did, too. Guess we were both wrong!"

"Allison, for cripes' sakes, what's wrong?"

"If you don't know, I'm not going to tell you," I said, and hung up. I was furious. Talk about chauvinistic. Talk about double standards. Talk about wanting to have your cake and eat it, too, as my father would have put it.

Without exaggeration, the next day had to be the worst day of my life. Everything went wrong, just everything, starting with the moment I woke up. First, I lost a contact lens and went totally bonkers trying to find it, terrified to tell my folks, sure they'd slaughter me, because those lenses had cost them a minor fortune, and after all they were practically brand new. I didn't say anything, and I just kept hunting for that lens, getting more paranoid by the second. Walking around with only one functional eye wasn't helping either. I was getting the world's worst headache. Finally, I went to my mom and confessed all. It turned out I hadn't even had to go through all that agonizing ordeal in the first place, since luckily, the stupid lenses were fully insured. We just had to go over to Dr. Koenig's office, where he fitted me for another one.

Susannah showed up, and we started working on the dress, both of us getting pretty frantic because we were working against time, and it was taking longer than we had thought. If that wasn't stressful enough, a call came from Andrea who said she was down with mononucleosis and was probably going to die. Whereupon, in a state of hysteria both my parents took off in the car, heading for the airport and a plane to Berkeley, promising faithfully they'd do their best to return in time for the concert, but adding that if their best wasn't good enough, I shouldn't be upset.

"Oh, right, I won't be upset," I muttered, heading back upstairs to my room, where Susannah was handstitching the lace trim on the pintucks on the bodice of the dress. "Why should I be upset? Nothing to be upset about! I always play solos in concerts. It's an everyday occurrence, so it's no big thing if my parents can't be there to see me."

Helga, the most thoughtful person in the world when the chips are down, came in with a tray with our lunch, chicken salad stuffed in avocado halves, toasted pita bread with sesame butter, and iced tea.

"Gosh, how elegant!" Susannah said, hugely impressed. "Could we ever use you at our house, Helga. Maybe then we'd get to eat a halfway decent meal."

"*Halfway* decent?" Helga sniffed, turning on her heel and marching downstairs, muttering to herself.

"I meant *gourmet* meal!" Susannah called after her, grinning at me. "Look, if it helps any, I'll be there for you tonight," she said, "and whether you want to believe it or not, so will Bobby."

"Well, maybe you'd better plan on driving me, just in case," I said, ignoring the last part of the remark.

The dress was finished by four, which left me a few hours to rest before I had to get dressed. Of course I didn't rest. I sat on my bed taking my frustrations and hostilities out on my trusty violin, under the guise of getting it in tune for the performance. My folks called and said Andrea was pretty sick, but that she would undoubtedly live to become Super Doctor as planned, and that they thought I'd better ask Susannah to drive me to school, just in case their plane was late.

"I already asked her. Don't worry. Just take it easy. Anytime you get there is all right. I'm just so relieved you're going to get there!" I said, falling all over myself with gratitude.

Not that I felt like making like a violin virtuoso, you understand. I mean, if I could have called Mr. Petrie and wangled my way out of it, I would have. I wasn't exactly thrilled about the prospect of getting up there in front of a whole auditorium full of people and being brilliantly gifted. Actually, what I really wanted to do was crawl under the covers and stick my thumb in my mouth.

Helga tried to get me to eat some dinner, but the thought of food at that point was revolting. I assured her I wouldn't die of malnutrition from skipping one meal.

"You're getting too skinny," she said, shaking her head disapprovingly at me. "I was saying that to your mother the other day. 'Allison's getting too skinny,' I said to her."

Too skinny? All my life I wanted someone to say that to me, that I was too skinny. I mean, can you imagine anything more wonderful, especially for someone who's spent her entire life being too fat?

I hopped into the shower, shampooed my hair, and then started to get dressed. Susannah showed up to help me with my makeup and make sure the dress was okay. She and Helga made this great big fuss over how gorgeous I looked, lavishing me with compliments until I told them if they said another word I'd throw up right then and there.

Susannah finally carted me away, a veritable basket case from sheer, unadulterated nervous hysteria.

"Are you going to be okay?" she said when we got to the auditorium.

"Yes, and believe me, this is not on account of playing a violin solo in a dopey school concert. Susannah, I'm so miserable!" I cried, throwing myself on her, starting to sob my heart out. "Why is this happening to me? What'd I do to deserve to be so unhappy?"

"Nothing," she sighed, then sounding a whole lot like me, she added, "You don't have to *do* anything to earn being unhappy. It just happens. Listen, you're going to mess up your makeup. Pull yourself together, okay? Do you want anything? A Coke maybe? Some tea? A glass of warm milk? Some arsenic?"

I couldn't help it. I laughed. Somehow Susannah just knew the exact right thing to say at the exact right time to pull you out of the doldrums. Mr. Petrie came dashing in, and if I thought *I* was hysterical, he was totally off the walls. He started yelling, "Allison! Allison! Where's Allison? Has anybody seen Allison?" while looking straight at me.

"Over here," I said, trying to keep a straight face.

"In ten minutes you're playing Brahms, and what are you doing? Standing here gossiping with your girlfriends!"

"Girl*friend*," I amended, glancing at Susannah, who made a face guaranteed to make an undertaker laugh, sending me into spasms of giggles.

"Wonderful! Just what I need," Mr. Petrie said, glaring at me. "A girl with the giggles playing Brahms."

Ms. Hartley came in to wish me luck. So did Mr. Nordstrom and Ms. Dorcas.

"Just what I need to put the finishing touch on a day to end all days," I muttered, looking at Susannah. Bobby came in, looking so gorgeous it took my breath away, in this midnight-blue corduroy suit with a white-on-white shirt and a striped tie. He stood there looking at me with this agonized expression. I just turned my back on him.

Susannah said "Give the poor boy a break," or something like that, but I just ignored her and went to collect my violin. I opened the case, took the violin out, and started tuning up, putting rosin on my bow, the usual routine. The members of the orchestra started straggling in. Mr. Petrie stood in the wings, looking as though he was going to collapse any minute. The commotion from the other side of the curtains indicated the auditorium was jampacked. I wanted to peek out to see if my folks had arrived, but I sat down in my place instead, resting my violin on my knee, glancing over to the woodwinds to see what Bobby was doing. What Bobby was doing was staring at me, which made me feel terrific. I looked away, pretending to be adjusting the bridge of my violin; doing anything but noticing him in all his masculine glory. Let him stew in his own juice (another of my father's all-time favorites). I wasn't going to make it easy for him.

Here I was, about to play a solo in the biggest

concert of the year, and I felt numb. All the effort Susannah and I had put into this, and it didn't matter to me anymore. Nothing mattered in fact. To tell the truth, if there had been some way I could have snuck off the stage, slipped away, and gone home, I would have. That's how down and depressed I was feeling.

Mr. Simon, our beloved principal, stepped out in front of the curtain and gave one of his chatty, informal speeches. When Mr. Simon gives a speech, chatty, informal, or otherwise, he always tries to sound like he's one of us kids, making with all the hip jargon. You know, using all these "in" phrases: "right on," "far out," "way to go."

The curtains parted. The audience applauded politely, and Mr. Petrie stalked out on the stage, moving like a robot. He took his place at the podium, this glazed expression in his eyes, like a man being led to his own execution. He tapped three times on the podium, raised his baton in the air, and gave the signal, and we launched into the Beatles medley, sounding like the entire Boston Pops orchestra, playing music to have your teeth drilled or ride an elevator by.

Halfway through the piece, someplace between "Got to Get You Into My Life" and "I Am the Walrus," I started to come to life, and by the time we reached my solo, I was one hundred percent there. I don't want to sound like the world's most conceited person, but I played great that night. I was so darned good, I even surprised *myself*. Later, when I thought about it, I realized why. Playing the violin that night was my own emotional catharsis, an outlet for all those pent-up feelings I was dealing with. Instead of letting them out some other way — having a tantrum, crying my eyes out, going on a talking jag, or sulking somewhere in a room all alone — I let it all out on my violin.

The consensus of opinion was I was the greatest violinist of all time. People kept coming back-stage, making this huge fuss over me, telling me how brilliantly talented I was, and how smashing I looked, and how I had been the highlight of this, or any other concert and would indubitably be a famous professional concert artist in the near future. I just stood there, trying to be properly appreciative and flattered, but all I wanted to do was go home, take off my clothes, crawl into my bed, and die.

I was walking out of the auditorium when I saw Bobby with his two older brothers, one sister, and his parents. He looked at me. I looked at him. We looked at one another for the longest time. I felt my heart shriveling up inside me. There was no doubt in my mind that this was good-bye for-ever. When he turned his back on me and walked away, I knew it was over.

—— 17 ——

"Don't you want to go out and celebrate?" my father said, taking my violin case from me and giving me a hug. "You're the star, after all."

"I really would just rather go straight home," I said, trying not to sound too tragic. He started rhapsodizing about my performance, sounding kind of surprised that I had been so good.

"I knew you were good, but I didn't realize you were *that* good. What an extraordinary talent! Mr. Petrie tells me you have the makings of a first-rate musician."

"Well, you didn't have to wait for Mr. Petrie to tell you. I could have told you that."

"I had no idea," he kept saying. "To think we have a violin virtuoso in the family."

"A violin virtuoso has to be totally dedicated. You're not all that dedicated, are you, Allison?" my mother asked, smiling at me.

I glanced at Susannah. She gave me a look as if to say, "Well? Why don't you say something, dummy?"

We were in the parking lot, walking to the car. It was dark, which was just as well, because I didn't want my parents to see my face. "Yes, I am, Mom," I said very softly. "Just to let you know just how dedicated I am, if I thought there was half a chance I could make it as a professional musician, I'd spend the rest of my life trying, even if it meant playing on street corners for pennies."

I waited for the bomb to drop, thinking I probably had the worst timing in the world, hitting them with it at an inauspicious time like this. Talk about being vulnerable! After what they had just been through with Andrea, they sure were, but then I reminded myself I was, too, so that made us even.

"Allison, if you feel that way, why haven't you ever said anything to us before?" my mother said, her hand on the handle of the car door.

I shrugged. "I knew how you'd react, that's all. I mean, to you two, playing the violin's a dandy hobby for anyone to have, but you don't think of it as a career."

My father got very busy unlocking the car door, climbing in behind the wheel, flipping the automatic lock switch to unlock the other doors. I could see by his face he was in shock, so I didn't say anything, figuring he probably needed a little time to adjust. Susannah and I climbed into the back seat, and my mom got in front next to my father. I saw him give her this pleading look, as if to say, "I can't handle this. You talk to her."

"The question is," she said, rising to the occasion as always, "not whether *we* want you to make a career of playing the violin, but whether *you* want to. It's not our future or our career, after all. It's yours."

I glanced at Susannah. "But what about being a doctor? That's always been pretty much taken for granted, that that's what I was going to do with my life."

"Has it?"

"Well, hasn't it? Come on, Mom. Don't tell me you and Daddy haven't counted on it, had your hearts set on Andrea and me being doctors, too, just like you two. It never occurred to you I might want to do something else with my life."

Susannah smiled encouragement. I shrugged, feeling a little panicked. Too late to turn back now and undo what I'd done. I'd opened my mouth and stuck my foot in it, and now I wasn't going to be able to take it back out all that easily.

My father backed the car out of the parking space, made a huge, cautious U-turn around the entire parking lot, then headed for the exit. Not until he was out on Greentree Lane did he say anything. What he said positively floored me. "The reason it never occurred to us you might want to do something else was you led us to believe being a doctor was what you wanted, too. It was taken for granted because you never once indicated otherwise. If you had, we would have been a little more enlightened on the subject, wouldn't we?"

"But I never came right out and said I was all that gung ho for devoting my life to science and medicine, did I?" I argued, remembering all the times I had. Susannah made a A-okay sign in the air with her thumb and forefinger. I shrugged, feeling surrounded. "I might have misled you, but only because I knew for a fact how heartbroken you'd be if I ever told you I wanted to pass on being a doctor in favor of something else."

"Heartbroken?" my mother said, turning around in her seat. "I wouldn't use that word exactly. Disappointed, perhaps, but heartbroken? No. I don't think so, dear. Becoming a violinist isn't exactly like going into the drug trade. If that's what you were planning on doing with your life, we might be heartbroken. Playing the violin? Well, that I think I can live with." She turned to my dad. "How about you, Harry? Do you think you can live with having a violinist for a daughter?"

"One violinist, one doctor. Maybe three doctors in one family is enough anyway," he said, smiling at me in the rearview mirror. "Allison, I'm hurt that you felt you couldn't confide in us before now. That you didn't know what our attitude would be."

"Hey, I'm sorry. I underestimated you. I know that now," I said, looking at Susannah, who was grinning from ear to ear. "You don't know how glad I am I finally told you about this. I would have had to sooner or later, and I'm glad it was sooner instead."

"Are you positive you don't want to go somewhere and celebrate?" my father said, and we all laughed. "There's this place I heard about, not far from here actually, where they supposedly have good live music. Now, what was the name? Something about a toothbrush . . ."

"The Sagebrush Cantina," Susannah put in. "The whole orchestra's going there to celebrate."

"Right! That's it, The Sagebrush Cantina. Why don't we go there and tear the place up? After all, we have something to celebrate. It isn't every night in the week our daughter decides to become a famous violin virtuoso!"

We went to The Sagebrush Cantina. It turned out, everybody else in the whole orchestra was there, too, with their families. I was afraid we'd run into Bobby, but Susannah said, "It's okay. He's not here. I looked."

"I'm not in the world's most jovial mood," I mumbled, following my folks to a table near the bandstand. "I really would have liked to have gone home."

"Why? So you could sit in your room and feel sorry for yourself? It's a special occasion. You owe yourself a celebration. You can feel sorry for yourself later."

It turned out to be an okay evening, if you like loud Mexican music and Mexican hat dances, and tacos so hot the inside of your mouth is still burning four days later. I guess I enjoyed myself to a degree, which probably just goes to prove that what my father is always saying is true, there's no use crying over spilled milk, or behind every cloud there's a silver lining, or misery loves company, or some such timeworn cliché.

We got home pretty late, about one A.M., and I fell into bed, feeling as though I could sleep for a week. Susannah called at eight o'clock to tell me she, Mitch, and Scott were just about to leave her house.

"Tell them you couldn't reach me," I moaned into the phone. "Tell them you called, and my father said I was still asleep. Tell them anything, Susannah. I can't do it."

"Get up! Get dressed. No excuses. You're coming with us to the beach!" she said, and hung up.

Somehow I managed to pull myself together. I must have looked like a basket case, but I wore sunglasses and that helped. Just in case I wasn't in bad enough shape, Scott turned out to be an octopus, all hands, and I had to spend the entire day fending him off.

"What's *with* this guy? Can't he take a hint?" I said to Susannah when she and I were taking a walk on the beach.

"Some guys think you don't really mean it when you say no; that if they hang in there, finally you'll give in. Listen, if you want to go home, Mitch says he'll be glad to take you. We feel kind of guilty. You didn't really want to come, and now you're having a crummy time."

"It's not your fault! I'm a big girl, aren't I? No, don't answer that. Listen, I can stick it out 'til the bitter end."

161

All the way home in the back of Mitch's pick-up, Scott kept it up, until finally I couldn't stand it anymore, so I said, "Just think of all the scores you could make the second time you go out with a girl, if only you wouldn't turn her off on the first." I think that did the trick. From that moment on, Scott kept all six pairs of hands to himself.

"Robert Redford called," Helga said when I got home.

"And who else?"

"Bobby, B. for Beautiful, Stern, among others."

"Oh! Well, uh, thanks," I said, and took off for my room. Should I call him back or shouldn't I? No matter what he had to say, I didn't want to hear it. On the other hand, what if he was calling to swear his undying love, to threaten suicide if I didn't take him back, to vow unwavering fidelity now and for always, and tell me he was never going to see Judy again?

I was still debating with myself when the phone rang. "Could I come over? I want to talk to you," Bobby said.

"Sure, but I don't think there's all that much to talk about, do you?"

"If I didn't, I wouldn't be coming over. Right?"

I took a quick shower, put on jeans and a halter, and met him at the door, trying to appear cool, calm, and collected.

"Want to go out back? I made some iced tea. It's pretty cool out there," I said, heading for the back patio.

He followed me outside. "I heard you were at

Zuma today," he said, slamming the back door so hard the pictures on the wall shook. "So, who was the guy you were with?"

"Boy, you sure have a dandy communications system! Who told you? There wasn't even anyone there we knew."

"Who was the guy, Allison?"

I shrugged. "His name's Scott. He's a friend of Mitch's."

"Who's Mitch?"

"A friend of Susannah's. I told you, they're in love."

"I thought Susannah was going with this guy Marc."

"She is, but she's going with Mitch, too," I made the mistake of saying. He looked at me, and I knew what he was thinking. I purposely didn't say anything to disprove the misconception. Let him think I was in love with someone else. It served him right if he was jealous.

"I heard you and this Scott were pretty chummy, too," he said.

"You're very well-informed."

"Look," he said, taking a step toward me. I shoved a glass of iced tea in his hand. "I can't figure what's going on," he said, and looked at it as though he was wondering how it got there. "What did I do, Allison? Why are you mad at me? It's crazy! One minute we're going steady. The next you're out with some other guy. What am I supposed to think?"

"Think whatever you like. I don't care what you think. Look, you've got some nerve questioning me about who I'm going out with. You're going out, so why shouldn't I?"

"Me? Going out? What are you talking about, Allison?"

"Oh, come on! I know about darling Judy. How could I not? All you do is talk about her."

"Judy?" He stood there, staring at me for a long moment, looking puzzled. Then he cried, "Judy? Oh, wow! Is that what you thought? That I was having a thing with *Judy*? I thought I told you about Judy. I did tell you about Judy, didn't I?"

"Told me and told me. Bobby, stop conning me, okay?" I said, getting angrier by the second.

"Conning you?" he said, reaching for my hand. I pulled it away, but he grabbed it anyway and held on tight. "Judy is a friend, a close friend," he said, smiling into my eyes. "We dig each other a lot, but as friends only . . ."

"Yeah, yeah, yeah. I've heard that one before," I groaned, trying to pull away. "Judy's just a friend, a platonic friend. Only, when I asked you to spend the day with me at the beach, you preferred to be with your platonic friend Judy."

"Allison, Judy and I already had made plans for the day. I wasn't about to disappoint her. I don't make a habit of doing things like that to my friends, and Judy, well, she means a whole lot to me . . ."

"I can tell!"

"Can you? Well, it's true. We have a very special relationship. Judy's a special person, too. She also happens to be beautiful, bright, charm-

164

ing, talented, and very loving. If not for the discrepancy in our ages, I'd probably decide to marry her, but Judy just happens to be sixty years old and very married, so I guess that's out."

I stood there staring at him for a moment. Then I cried, "Oh, Bobby!" and threw myself into his arms, nearly knocking him into a pot of flowering pink impatiens in my earnestness. "Bobby, I'm so sorry! How could I be such a dummy? I wouldn't blame you if you never spoke to me again after the way I acted. You didn't deserve to be treated so shabbily."

"Hey, I understand," he said, hugging me, and I knew he did. "I know how your mind works. I should have known what you were thinking. I would have explained, only it never occurred to me I hadn't already; that you didn't know all about Judy. Look, just let's not let a thing like this happen again. Okay? Next time you've got something on your mind, spit it out and we'll talk. There shouldn't be any misunderstandings between us. Not between two people as close as we are."

"We *are* close," I mused, reaching up to kiss him lightly on the lips. "So close I should have known. I was just so miserable, I can't tell you. It was awful. I don't know how I made it through that concert. I was at such an all-time low. I thought it was over and I couldn't bear it."

I told him about the awful day I had had, about my parents having to take off for Berkeley on account of Andrea's mononucleosis, about the lost contact lens, and finally about my telling my

165

parents about not wanting to be a doctor. He hugged me when he heard that part and said, "See? You were way off base about that, too. If you'd said something to them before, you would have saved yourself a lot of worry. It just goes to prove, honesty's the best policy. You're always so gung ho about this honesty thing, but when the chips were down, you weren't being honest, and all it did for you was make trouble."

"Exactly what Susannah kept telling me," I said. "I should have listened to her. I promise," I went on, giving him another hug, "from now on, as my dear old dad would say, what's on my mind will be on my tongue."

"Well, let's not get carried away," Bobby laughed, kissing me. "There's such a thing as being *too* honest, in case you haven't heard."

Bobby drove me to Susannah's so she could be the first to hear the news.

"We made up," I said when she opened the front door. "I knew you'd want to be the first to know, Cupid baby."

She grinned, looking a little embarrassed, and said, "Listen, don't knock it. If I hadn't played Cupid, you guys would still be suffering in silence, in love at a distance. I've got something to tell you, too, by the way," she said, whipping out a letter and handing it to me. "Read it out loud, will you?" she sighed, closing her eyes, looking ecstatic. "I never tire of hearing it."

" '*Dear Ms. Ellis*,' " I read, squinting at the page in the dimly lit hallway, " '*This is to inform you*

*that you have won second prize in our Designers
of the Future Contest'* . . . Oh, my gosh! Susannah,
you won," I squealed, throwing the letter in the
air and leaping on her. "I told you you would! I
told you, didn't I? You were so sure you didn't
have a chance, you ninny, and look. Second
prize. I wonder who won first, Gloria Vanderbilt,
Jr.? Bobby, do you know what this means?" I
said, hugging him, too. "This means Susannah
Ellis is going to be a famous fashion designer,
that's what it means. A few years from now,
everybody who's anybody'll be wearing a Susannah Ellis original, and paying a mint in money for
it, too."

"Yeah, yeah, yeah. How the girl does carry on,"
Susannah said, looking at Bobby.

"Read the rest of the letter," Susannah said,
shaking her head at me. "You always get so
emotional!"

"What's not to get emotional about? How come
you're not freaking out, Susannah?"

"I'm totally numb, that's why. I don't believe
it yet."

I read the rest of the letter. It explained about
the scholarship, which amounted to plenty of
money, but it stipulated that unless Susannah was
able to improve her overall grades markedly by
graduation, she wouldn't be eligible to receive it.

"Maybe that's why I'm not freaking out," she
said with a shrug. "I'm afraid to, because of *that*."

"Hey," I said, shaking my finger under her
nose, "Remember? No negative nonsense anymore, not for either of us. You proved you can do

167

it. It's not going to be a problem. You've got me, haven't you? We're The Dynamic Duo, aren't we? Together we can't miss!"

"You're going to spend the next year tutoring me in every subject? Allison, that's taking on a lot!"

"What's such a lot? Listen, it's no big deal, and besides I enjoy it. We're together all the time, right? So? No hassle!"

—— 18 ——

Next morning, at six-forty-five sharp, Susannah showed up at my door, resplendent in her new jogging suit, violet-blue to match her eyes.

"You've got to be kidding," I groaned, peering out at her. Without my contacts, all I could see was a violet-blue blur. "I'm in no condition to jog today. Not after that weekend. Not after last night!"

"Come on. Remember what today is?"

"Oh, gosh. Right! I almost forgot. How thoughtless of me." I raced upstairs and jumped into a sweatsuit. How I was going to jog was beyond me. I figured I'd die trying, though. After all, was I a steadfast and loyal friend, or wasn't I?

On our way into the hills, we planned our strategy. It started to drizzle. Then just at the exact moment when we separated, I jogging off in one direction, Susannah in another, it began to pour.

Inside of thirty seconds, I was drenched to the skin.

It's an omen! I thought apprehensively. Let me tell you, whoever said it never rains in southern California had to be from the east. It doesn't just rain. It pours! Where do you run for cover when you're out jogging, and it starts to rain all over you? Unless you've got friends in the neighborhood, nowhere. I just kept jogging along, figuring at this point I was soaked to the skin and couldn't very well get wetter, so what did it matter? I was pretty nervous. I kept checking my watch, thinking that after going through her ordeal, I didn't want Susannah to arrive at our prearranged place and not find me there, waiting to console her.

I headed back five minutes early, but Susannah was fifteen minutes late. *At this rate,* I thought, *if I didn't have double pneumonia by morning, it would be a miracle.* Susannah finally showed up, not jogging; walking. She looked as though she had just gone ten rounds with Muhammad Ali.

"How did it go?" I asked, all tender solicitude. She shrugged. "Not too bad."

"How did he take it? Was he desolate? Did he get down on one knee and beg and plead or what?"

"More like his ego got a little soggy and wrinkled. He'll get over it, maybe in about ten minutes. I must be totally bonkers, breaking up with someone who looks like that, drives a Mercedes 250 SL, lives in a mansion, and has his own swimming pool and tennis court in the backyard."

"Don't forget the movie studio and the screening room, oh, and the indoor raquetball court," I murmured, smiling at her.

"All right, all right, I get the message."

We got to Ventura Boulevard across the street from Solly's, and I was suddenly ravenous, so I said, "Hey, let's have brunch, okay? My treat."

Without breaking our rhythm, the two of us jogged across the street. I held up my hand like a policeperson directing traffic. Susannah waved to a pedestrian and made the peace sign at a bunch of young guys in an ancient pickup truck. Still jogging, we headed in through the double doors of Solly's, right past the cashier, right past Solly himself, right over to our usual table, dripping buckets every inch of the way, making pools of water all over Solly's nice, clean, freshly scrubbed floor.

When our orange juice came, I lifted my glass and said, "To you and Mitch."

Susannah grinned and lifted hers. "To you and Bobby."

I clicked my glass against hers. "May we all live happily every after . . . as my father would say."